If I Die Before I Wake

Martii Maclean

*For **Trevor** and **Minerva**,
my best buddies and greatest supporters.*

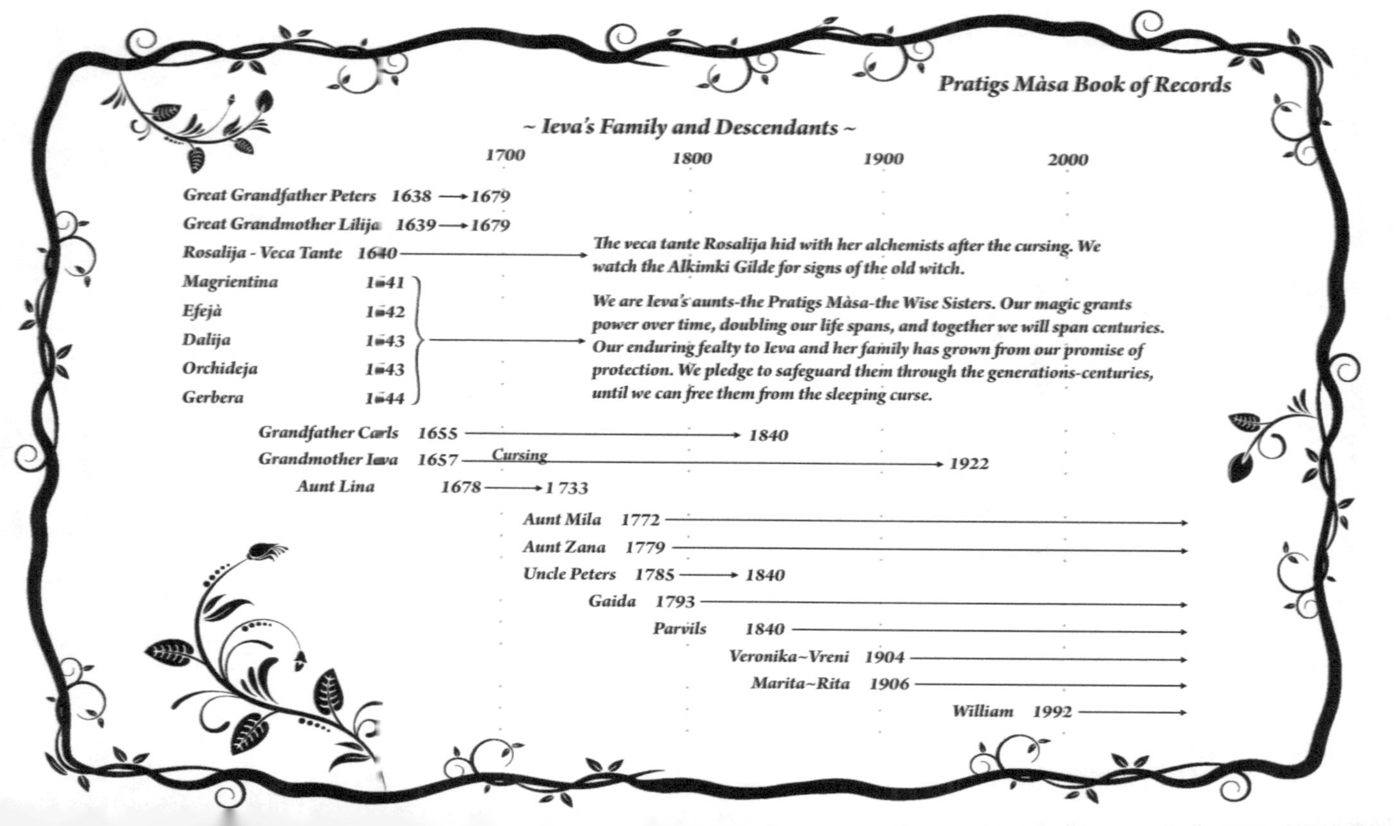

Pratigs Màsa Book of Records

~ Ieva's Family and Descendants ~

1700   1800   1900   2000

Great Grandfather Peters   1638 ⟶ 1679
Great Grandmother Lilija   1639 ⟶ 1679
Rosalija - Veca Tante   1640 ⟶

The veca tante Rosalija hid with her alchemists after the cursing. We watch the Alkimki Gilde for signs of the old witch.

Magrientina   1641
Efejà   1642
Dalija   1643
Orchideja   1643
Gerbera   1644

We are Ieva's aunts-the Pratigs Màsa-the Wise Sisters. Our magic grants power over time, doubling our life spans, and together we will span centuries. Our enduring fealty to Ieva and her family has grown from our promise of protection. We pledge to safeguard them through the generations-centuries, until we can free them from the sleeping curse.

Grandfather Carls   1655 ⟶ 1840
Grandmother Ieva   1657   Cursing ⟶ 1922
Aunt Lina   1678 ⟶ 1733

Aunt Mila   1772 ⟶
Aunt Zana   1779 ⟶
Uncle Peters   1785 ⟶ 1840
Gaida   1793 ⟶
Parvils   1840 ⟶
Veronika~Vreni   1904 ⟶
Marita~Rita   1906 ⟶
William   1992 ⟶

Litany

Veca Tante and her alchemists have cursed the Lady Ieva and presume her lost to the darkness of the sleeping death. But we Pratigs Māsa, the Wise Sisters, have softened the potion. Ieva sleeps and wakes at the whim of the curse, as does her newly born daughter. And so, we fear, will her grand daughters. These sleeping beauties need protection from Veca Tante and the world. We pledge to watch over them for as long as the curse may last.
~ Pratigs Māsa, *Book of Wisdoms*

Vreni woke with a shudder. Her heart sprang to life within her chest as though it was a wild creature released from its bindings. Her body tensed in response to the searing pain of her first breath as it entered her long-dormant lungs, which had remained so still during her long-sleep. She wondered if this was why newborn babies cried: this burning breath.

The magical bindings of the curse held Vreni's body frozen for a few more frightening moments. She concentrated on calming her breathing and waited. With each fluttering squeeze of her heart, blood pumped through her body and sent a sensation like burning needles radiating outward in a wave of fiery pain. She tensed again, forcing a breath through her clenched teeth while she flexed her rigid muscles, hoping to speed up the painful transition out of long-sleep.

Her litany always began the same way. 'I am Vreni. I am fifteen years old.' *This is my twentieth awakening. Or am I one hundred? How much time had passed during her long-sleep this time?*

The heat in her lungs began to cool. The burning pain moved down her arms and legs, and then faded, as if flowing out from her toes and fingertips. She stretched slowly, feeling as though she was made of rock.

'I am Vreni. I am fifteen years old. My mother is Gaida; my father is Parvils. Peters was my brother. My younger sister is Rita.' *Or is she my older sister now? Have we both slept? Am I the little sister again? She knew she was still younger than Mama, but maybe one day she would not be. She would always be younger than Papa.*

'Papa!' Her heart tightened into a fist. *Is Papa still alive? Of course he is, or I would already know.*

'Don't fret, sweet one, I'm here,' said her father's muddy voice.

Vreni opened her green eyes. She was so grateful that he was always there when she woke from long-sleep. He looked a little greyer now, and there seemed to be the slightest frailness in his voice. But perhaps he'd always been old like this and she'd just been too young to notice before now.

Of course her father was old. Vreni watched her father's amulet swinging on its chain as he leaned over her. It glinted in the narrow strip of morning light that slipped through the heavy curtains. She reached out and touched the warm silver. Her father had worn this amulet ever since the day he had married her mother, nearly one hundred and fifty years ago.

The amulet was full of magic. The Pratigs Māsa, the Wise Sisters, used the old magic to slow the effects of time on Parvils so he could live three or even four normal lifetimes while he watched over the sleepers he loved, including Vreni.

Not all the men in the family had received the magical gift of power over time. This charm was only given to those who chose freely, knowingly and out of love, to pledge themselves to the family.

Sons were never sleepers. No such charm was ever offered to a male child, but it was given to those who chose freely, knowingly and out of love to pledge themselves to the family as Parvils had done when he married Gaida. Families had to watch their sons grow to manhood and through to brittle old age and death in front of their eyes. This is what had happened to Vreni's brother Peters. She remembered waking to hear the cries of anguish the day he died.

Even though the Wise Sisters had softened the sleeping potion and removed much of the evil and hatred, a horrible cruelty remained: the curse woke the sleepers briefly to feel the pain and loss when a loved one died. Vreni, along with her sister, mother and aunties, had woken when her brother died, but they didn't remain awake long enough to find solace through singing at his funeral. They could only weep for him until the long-sleep of the curse recaptured them.

Her father brushed a dark strand of hair from her face.

'How did you know to be here?' she asked. 'How do you know when we will wake?'

He smiled and shrugged. 'When you've waited as long as I have, you develop a sense for it, a knowing.'

She hugged him to her. He felt frail; he was smaller somehow, she was sure of it. 'How long this time?' she asked.

'It's been three years. Rita has slept too, so you're still the oldest, for the moment ...'

When Vreni was younger, long-sleep had been confusing. She would wake up expecting familiarity and comfort, but instead see unsettling changes: the people she knew always looked just a little different.

She was the first-born daughter, but, as she discovered, in her family age and birthdays did a strange dance around each other. She remembered waking once to see her younger sister Rita, a rosy-faced baby girl, sitting on the hearth rug in front of a cosy fire. Rita had laughed delightedly when Vreni rolled a ball to her. The ball had been crocheted from brightly coloured yarns.

At Vreni's next awakening she again rolled the ball toward Rita, but the ball was faded with age and she herself was older. At first the ball and Rita felt strange to Vreni, but she also felt acceptance—intuition more than understanding—

and had snuggled into this older Rita's arms to listen to her tell a story while she toyed with the faded ball.

'Three years,' Vreni echoed. 'And while we slept have we all been moved again to another strange country?'

'No, we haven't moved again.' Her father looked wounded by her words.

She knew the question had been unfair and she wished she had spoken more thoughtfully. Her father sometimes had to make hard decisions to keep the family safely hidden.

She had once woken to find everything changed. Her home was gone. The family had left Vārve and moved thousands of kilometres away from everything she knew. The journey had taken many months, but to Vreni it had happened in the blink of an eye between sleeping and waking.

I'm acting like a child. I wouldn't want the burden Papa carries. 'That was thoughtless of me, Papa,' she said. 'Forgive me.'

'Always,' he whispered.

Her family had been hidden from the world in one way or another since the time of the cursing, over three hundred years previously. Each new tutor the Wise Sisters sent had taught Vreni pieces of the family history, but to her young ears it sounded like a fanciful tale about other people, in other places. But as she grew older she began to comprehend the sleeping curse and what the life of a sleeper was like.

She accepted that this was her story, too. She would have to live as a sleeper, but what did that really mean?

So far it had meant isolation, and, as she grew older, restlessness, since her family insisted on staying hidden from the world. *Maybe during my awakening this time Papa will say yes, and I'll get to go somewhere. Anywhere.*

Her father stood up next to her bed and smiled down at her. 'Good morning, *Lady Veronika*,' he said, using her full name. 'Welcome back among us.' He kissed her hand and bowed like a servant. It was a quaint ritual that had been part of her waking from long-sleep ever since she was very young.

'You'll be hungry when your stomach awakens,' he said. 'I'll see to breakfast.' He squeezed her hand and left the room.

The burning and aching had almost faded from her body. She sat up slowly, feeling a slight dizziness. Stretching out her legs, she wiggled her toes in the plush rug beside her bed. The light-headedness returned for a moment as she stood. She walked across the warm wooden floor, flexing her arms and legs to melt away the last of the stiffness.

Reaching the tall window, she pushed the heavy curtains open and stared out at the dazzling blue of the sea; it seemed to go on forever, fading into the horizon. Closing her eyes, she let the morning sun warm her, melting away the last chills of long-sleep. Then she pushed open the windows and breathed in the fresh salty air. Her lungs crinkled painfully as she forced them to expand fully.

She never tired of watching the ocean. They had lived next to the sea back in Vārve, but here the light was stronger and the water was almost always blue. Many things were different here. Papa had found this remote clifftop house and renovated it until he was sure it would delight his family. He knew it *had* to delight them, because they never left it.

There were many rooms in the rambling house to accommodate the family and staff. A library for Papa, a large kitchen, a conservatory where they had their lessons, and her favourite: the tower, which rose up from the centre of the house. It was a place that was just for Vreni and Rita. Papa had built the tower so they could look out over the 'world', even if their world was only the gardens, the cliffs and the ocean beyond.

She closed her eyes against the glare, feeling the salt breeze on her face.

I am awake again.

Ever After

~ Ieva's private journal

Vreni stretched once more, took a deep, pain-free breath and wandered over to her closet. The clothes had changed so much throughout her century: tight bodices, skirts and petticoats had become stiff woollen jackets and strange little hats, which then became mini skirts and high heels. Vreni had collected fashion souvenirs from each awakening.

'My favourite things from my favourite decades,' she whispered, taking out faded jeans, a mohair cardigan, and a T-shirt with a smiling yellow face on the front.

When she was dressed she draped a floral silk scarf around her neck and looked at herself in the mirror.

'You look like a gypsy,' Rita said, walking through the half-open door.

'Papa didn't tell —' Vreni hugged her sister excitedly.

'You're right, I didn't tell you that the fair Lady Marita was awake and with us too,' Papa said to Vreni, laughing, as he stepped through the door. 'You know I like surprises, my darlings.'

'And Mama?' Vreni said.

It was as though a small cloud moved across her father's face. 'She always sleeps longer than you girls,' he said. 'The curse must be becoming diluted with the generations, or maybe my daughters are obstinate and refuse even to be cursed properly.' He smiled.

Vreni threw her balled-up socks at him.

'Breakfast is ready,' he said with a laugh, and pulled the door closed behind him.

Rita sat next to Vreni on the bed, twisting a strand of her sister's hair around her finger, forming a lose ringlet. Then Rita fidgeted with her own hair, which was copper coloured like their mother's. Both had their father's green eyes, but Vreni had soft dark curls like Papa, except that his were always smoothed down.

'How was your waking?' Rita asked, forming another ringlet.

'It hurt, a lot, like it always does.'

'It's a shame the Wise Sisters couldn't have taken away the pain when they softened Grandmama's curse,' Rita said, hugging Vreni tightly.

They both knew it was sometimes hard to lighten the dark mood that lingered after waking from long-sleep. Veca Tante had put shadowy things in the potion, and not even the combined magic of all of Grandmama Ieva's other aunties could remove all the blackness when the curse was softened.

'Sunshine will help,' Rita said, leading Vreni back to the window. 'Maybe Papa's right and the curse *is* weakening.'

'Wouldn't it be great if the curse weakened and disappeared,' Vreni said. 'Then we could stop hiding and have a life.'

'Well, it hasn't happened in more than three hundred years, so don't get your hopes up. And this life is fine,' Rita said. 'We get to do anything we like.'

'Anything but leave here,' Vreni said. She sighed and forced a smile. 'How long have you been awake?'

'A few weeks,' Rita said. 'I've learned a new thing on the computer. There's a way to shop and order things. You should see what I've been buying.'

'Have you been doing *other* lessons?'

'Yeah, worse luck, but Sabina's back again, so it's okay.'

'Have you asked her about going out? About leaving the grounds and maybe going to the city?'

'I hinted at it, and I reminded her that you'd asked her the last time you were awake, but I think she pretended not to hear me.'

'She does that to me, too,' Vreni said. 'We'll just have to try harder.'

'Vreni, it's not that bad. We have everything, and if we don't I can just order it for us. Papa hardly ever says no as long as I address everything care of the family trust so they look like business deliveries. That way the postmistress doesn't ask nosy questions when Uncle Artūrs picks up the packages.'

'But this *isn't* everything, Rita. Don't you ever want to go anywhere?' Vreni snapped. 'It's not like Veca Tante's out there somewhere waiting for us. No magic could keep someone alive for centuries.'

'Are you sure, Vreni? No one knows what happened to her.'

'That's enough fairytales, Rita. They just use that as an excuse to stop us going anywhere.'

Rita sighed. 'You're just grumpy after long-sleep.' She rubbed Vreni's hand. 'We do get to go places. We go to the beach a lot, and we can take the ponies.'

'Yes, I love riding, especially on the beach, but ... nothing ever really changes.' *My family might be magical, but I never see any magic.*

Her family might live by the magical rules of the sleeping curse, but for Vreni life was sheltered, predictable and boring. There were no surprises, which meant there were few choices that weren't already made for her. She wanted to make her own choices: to take chances sometimes.

Rita broke into her thoughts. 'At least we don't sleep as long as Mama,' she chirped.

'Mama! I must say good morning.'

Vreni left the room and walked quietly to her mother's room. 'Good morning, Mama,' she said, kissing Gaida on the forehead.

Rita appeared beside her and did the same thing.

'Mama still isn't awake. How does Papa endure it?' Vreni said.

'Well, for now he has us, so let's go and distract him.' Rita smiled mischievously.

At the top of the stairs Vreni stopped and looked over the railing into the foyer below. She winked at Rita and boosted herself up onto the banister rail. She hung there for a moment in anticipation before letting herself go. She slid on the smooth, polished wood all the way to the bottom of the stairs, her stomach lurching.

'Good to see you're feeling more like yourself now,' Rita said, running down the stairs after her.

Vreni's stomach caught up with her at the bottom of the stairs, as did Rita. They linked arms and walked quickly across to the kitchen, pushing the swinging door wide as they entered the warm, delicious-smelling room.

Parvils looked up from his breakfast and gestured towards a plate of eggs and cheese, and another of thinly sliced blackbread.

'My ladies,' he said, smiling warmly. 'Sit. Eat. It's so nice to hear happy noise in the house again.' He pushed a cardboard box towards them. 'But maybe you prefer porridge.'

'This is porridge?' Vreni said, turning the mysterious package around in her hands.

'*Instant* porridge, apparently.' Parvils' smile broadened. 'Obviously the people who made it have a different idea of what instant means than we do.'

'Well, we don't see much abracadabra around here ourselves, but do I need to call up the old magic to get instant porridge?' Vreni asked.

'No, just the microwave,' Rita said, pointing at the appliance.

Vreni shrugged. 'It's nice to see you're so comfortable with these new gadgets, but I'll have an egg.'

'I checked on the computer, Papa,' Rita said as she removed the shell from her boiled egg, 'and the weather's mild today. We could ride, all three of us.'

'Or pack a picnic and hike down the cliffs to the beach,' suggested Vreni.

'We could enjoy some time outside together today,' Papa agreed. 'Perhaps we could take a walk in the gardens before Sabina's lessons start.'

'Lessons *today*?' Vreni spluttered. 'But I just woke up.'

'Papa, it's our first day together,' Rita said. 'Surely you want to spend time with your daughters.'

'Life must go on as normal,' Papa said firmly.

'Normal,' Vreni said bitterly. To Papa, normal meant lessons, walks in the garden, trivial amusements, and endless reasons for never going anywhere.

Parvils looked at Vreni, holding her gaze for a long moment. 'Very well, if your legs are awake enough we can hike down the trail and take a picnic, maybe the ponies if Artūrs has time. I'll call Sabina and reschedule lessons for two o'clock.'

'But Papa—' Vreni and Rita protested in unison.

'They,' Parvils began and then quickly corrected himself, '*Sabina* insisted on starting your lessons again immediately.

She said she didn't want to waste time.' He returned stiffly to his breakfast.

Vreni watched him for a moment, wondering what was going on. *Who had Papa meant by 'they'? Why was it so urgent to have lessons?*

Sabina's lessons had changed during the last few awakenings. When she was alone with Sabina there seemed to be much less of the usual history and literature now, and more herblore and similar lessons. Those separate lessons felt strange, like she was viewing them from the corner of her eye and couldn't quite see, or remember, what she learned.

And then there were the strange dreams that always followed the lessons: a mishmash of voices chanting, and pungent aromas and a storm of images. Vreni always woke from them feeling confused and unsettled. She shivered as she remembered her dreams.

'You like catching up on all the gossip with Sabina,' Parvils said, too cheerfully. 'She'll be here soon enough, so eat up. Let's not waste a minute.'

Beach

All things of the earth and from the earth
have their nature that cannot be changed:
only accepted. True wisdom is to see that
our own nature is no more easily changed
than any other thing, but things can be
understood and used to their best purpose.
~ Book of Forest Lore

Within the hour they had left the symmetry of the manicured gardens that surrounded the house and started along the narrow path leading down to an isolated strip of beach. Parvils followed behind, carrying the picnic things.

The ragged cliff face showed layers of rock worn bare from eons of erosion and exposure by the ravages of wind and ocean storms. The cliff-side trail was steep, and wound in and out of pockets of lush rainforest.

Vreni stopped at an opening in the forest and stood on the very edge of the cliff, looking down as the waves hit the rocks below and surged upward in a forceful explosion of spray. She took hold of a scrawny tree and leaned out over the edge, feeling gravity pulling on her body. She imagined flying, and wondered if the tree would break or its roots pull free from where it clung to the rocky ground.

Not knowing what might happen captivated her. She hung there, watching the waves smash against the rocks. She felt the tree flexing with her weight, heard it quietly creak under the strain ...

'Vreni, surely you're not in *that* big a hurry to get to the bottom,' her father said from behind her.

'No, Papa.' She sighed and returned to the path. She walked on down the damp cliff track in silence.

Rita was right. Apart from things they had no power over, like the curse, or being forced to leave Vārve during wartime, her life was good. She and Rita lived like princesses. But now Vreni wanted to be part of the real world. She didn't want to just look at the world from the tower, or on Rita's computer.

The beach was a blinding mass of sparkling light bouncing off the blue-green water. They stopped at the end of the path and removed their shoes, tying the laces together and slinging them around their necks. Their feet sank into the warm sand. Each step they took squeaked as the grains of sand rubbed against each other. They shuffled through the grains, creating a tuneless song until they reached the damp sand nearer the water.

Without speaking they turned southward, as they always did. Vreni wished her mother were here too. *How long had it been since they were all together?* Her breath caught in her throat.

She took Papa and Rita by the hand and felt her throat relax. They continued along the beach together, following the random, curving line of foam left by the receding waves.

Vreni found a creamy, smooth shell and picked it up, brushing the sand away. 'Is this one good enough to be our keepsake for today?' She held it out to Rita and her father.

They always took one shell home and placed it a glass bowl as a record of their days together on the beach. Back in Vārve they had collected pebbles, and now they enjoyed keeping up the tradition with shells.

'This one is fine,' Papa said, taking the shell. 'Rita?' She nodded, so he placed it in his trouser pocket. 'Let's turn back and find a place to make camp.'

Their father sounded like an explorer, but Vreni knew that he would 'um' and 'ah' until he found a suitable position, then he would arrange the blanket and bags of picnic things, all the while looking very thoughtful. Then he would take off his button-up shirt, displaying a white singlet and even whiter skin. Then he would roll up his trouser legs to his knees. It seemed this was about as adventurous as her father ever got.

'Will you choose a good place for us, Papa?' Rita said, smiling at Vreni.

They turned to walk back and noticed a far-off figure at the end of the strip of sand. The sound of hammering echoed down the beach.

'Too bad,' Papa said, 'looks like we'll have to share the beach today. Maybe we should offer the stranger some help.' Without another word he started jogging up the beach.

Rita laughed. 'Papa's so funny. How many years has he been playing that stranger trick?'

Vreni smiled. 'Well, it might be years since Papa told us that joke, but only weeks, maybe months, since we last heard it. Remember to look surprised. Papa and Artūrs still act like we're five years old.'

The girls followed their father along the beach, thoroughly amused. The sight of him running, even slowly, was quite a novelty.

As they approached the two men they played their part, looking surprised to see Uncle Artūrs. He was leading their two ponies from the float at the rear of his truck.

'Oh Papa, Uncle Artūrs, what a great surprise,' Rita said.

Vreni squeezed her father's arm. 'Thank you.'

'I thought you'd enjoy a ride before lessons,' he said.

'Caramel, have you missed me?' Rita kissed the tan pony's muzzle and patted her smooth neck.

Vreni looked at the deep brown face of her pony. 'You're not my Chocolate Soufflé, are you?' she whispered. 'But you're still beautiful.'

'Very observant, Vreni,' Papa said. 'No, these ponies aren't *Caramel* or *Chocolate*.'

'They're their daughters,' added Artūrs proudly. 'Fudge and Crackle.'

'They were born a few years ago. We trained them while you were sleeping,' Papa explained.

'So, do you like your father's clever names? You know, Caramel *Fudge* and Chocolate *Crackle*.' Artūrs tapped his finger against the side of his head. 'Your papa is a clever man.'

'Absolutely, Papa.' Vreni hugged her father tightly.

'Well, don't keep the ponies waiting,' Artūrs said.

The girls took the ponies' reins, and with a boost up they were sitting high on their smooth, bare backs. With a soft tap of a heel, the excited ponies trotted off along the water's edge. Their hooves made gentle splashing sounds as they moved through the shallows and each girl got to know her pony's moods.

Vreni sat tall on Crackle's back. The deep-brown mane flicked against her hands as they rode into the breeze.

'Let's go, Crackle.' She gave Crackle a firm nudge in the flanks, and the pony cantered down the beach. Each hoof-fall in the shallow surf sent up fine splashes of cool water onto Vreni's legs.

Vreni saw that Fudge and Rita had come alongside, so she dug in her heels and Crackle lit off down the beach. She gripped the pony with her legs and took a tighter grip on the reins. She could hear Rita catching up behind her and felt Crackle's excitement grow.

Vreni leaned forward. 'Let's beat Rita to the end of the beach,' she called over the noise of hooves splashing in the foamy water.

Crackle snuffled her pleasure and breathed deeply; Vreni could feel the large ribcage expand under her. The pony let out an excited whinny and took off along the sand.

The wind buffeted Vreni's ears as she raced down the beach. Crackle's hooves made thumping, heartbeat sounds on the wet sand as she moved from a canter into a rhythmic gallop. Vreni leaned in close to her neck, smelling the salty mix of the sea air and the pony's sweat. Her heart danced in her chest. Her skin prickled with the heat of excitement.

Rita tried to pull ahead of them, but Crackle surged in front, enjoying the chance to be free, as did Vreni. She breathed deeply the adrenaline of this moment, the unfamiliarity of the new pony.

Without warning, Crackle stopped abruptly and reared up. She thumped her hooves down on the sand, changed direction and moved back into the water. Vreni, caught off guard by the sudden change of direction, began to lose her balance. Crackle waded out into deeper water and skittered playfully as the cold waves tickled her belly.

Vreni gripped harder with her legs, but it was too late. She slipped sideways, and as Crackle gave one last squirm of delight, Vreni plunged into the surf. The unexpected cold of the water forced a groan of surprise from her lungs. A small wave broke over her head, washing her hair over face.

She cleared the tangles from her eyes and felt the playful nudge of Crackle's nose rubbing up against her cheek. 'So now you're my rescuer, hey?'

Vreni stood up in the waist-deep water and the soft swell rocked her and pushed her against Crackle's shoulder. Crackle's eyes sparkled playfully, and the pony shook her head as if mocking Vreni.

'You look pretty happy for someone who just got thrown off her horse,' Rita called from the water's edge.

'Crackle surprised me,' Vreni said. 'She has a restless soul.'

'Just like her rider,' teased Rita. 'Does this mean I win?'

'Maybe,' Vreni said, leading Crackle back out of the water.

Rita came closer and offered a hand so Vreni could climb back up.

'Thanks, Rita.' Vreni sat dripping and smiling on Crackle's back. 'First one to lunch is the winner.' She kicked Crackle's flanks and galloped up the beach to where Parvils and Artūrs sat on a deep-blue blanket, leaning again two smooth rocks.

'We trained Crackle to dump you like that, you know,' Parvils said, laughing, as the girls tied up the ponies.

Parvils and Artūrs had begun eating already, and were congratulating themselves on the pony-breeding project. The blanket was covered with bowls and plates that contained chicken, potato salad dressed with sour cream, meat-filled pastries called pīrāgi and rye bread. There was also a small tray of cheese and dill cucumber. Vreni knew the round tin contained sweet apple bread to go with the milky coffee they would have later.

'Come, eat, we have a feast,' Parvils urged.

They had barely finished lunch when Parvils looked at his watch. 'We should brush down the ponies and get back up to the house.'

'That's it,' Vreni whispered into Crackle's ear as she brushed the pony's neck. 'Back to the corral for us both.'

Vreni brooded on the way back to the house. She knew she was returning to the tedium that trapped her. She longed for not knowing what might happen next, like when Crackle had thrown her into the surf, or when she had held herself out over the cliff edge, wondering if the spindly tree would break. Vreni wanted to go somewhere, do something, *anything* but the ever-after of lessons and time-filling drolleries.

Sabina's car followed the truck as it turned into the grounds and stopped at the front door.

'Stop here, ' Parvils said to Artūrs, waving at the tutor. 'I want to speak to Sabina. You go on and settle the ponies, girls. Then tidy yourselves and get ready for your lessons.' He got out of the truck and walked stiffly toward Sabina.

From outside the stables, Vreni watched what looked like an argument between Sabina and their father. Even from a distance, the tension between them was evident. Their raised voices drifted on the breeze, but Vreni couldn't hear anything but the emotional tone of their discussion.

Lessons

The young Veronika is showing great potential;
she could be the one. Continue with her
instruction in the old magic, but hide it from
her until we're certain she is the one.

~ Instructions to Sister Sabina

Sabina showed no sign of the mysterious argument with their father when the girls met her in the conservatory.

'Hi, Sabina,' Rita said.

'Hello, Sabina.' Vreni hugged the tall, dark-haired woman warmly. 'I'm glad it's you again.'

'I'm so pleased you've woken, Vreni,' Sabina said gently. 'And you're both awake together. That's wonderful for you.'

'So tell me all the gossip,' Vreni said, trying to delay the start of lessons.

'Let's have some tea and a *little* gossip, and then lessons,' Sabina said. A flash of seriousness crossed her face before she smiled and took the girls by the hand.

They sat on cane chairs at the end of the conservatory, beside the tea tray. Lessons had always been an inevitable part of Vreni's life, but in truth she enjoyed the company of a tutor, especially when her mother slept so long. Sabina made them work hard, but she also tried to help fill the gap when she noticed that the two sisters were missing their mother.

Once Vreni was old enough to be curious, each of her tutors, sent by the Wise Sisters, had also become her link to the world, especially before there was the internet. She loved seeing how the world of women had changed while she slept. The tutor's clothing was always different, along with the outside world.

'Sabina, your dress is beautiful,' complimented Rita.

'Thank you.'

'Did you buy it *online*?' Rita asked, sounding proudly expert on the topic.

'Online? Please tell me you're using that computer for study and not shopping,' Sabina said.

'Well, I had some time on my own, and I was bored. You should see what I ordered last week, Vreni. The parcels should arrive any day,' Rita said.

'I know I've only been asleep three years, but apart from Rita's shopping what changed during that time?' Vreni asked Sabina. 'What's new? Has anything amazing happened? Have they gone to the moon again?' She laughed. She always asked this question.

Sabina smiled. 'No, no one's been to the moon lately.'

They shared questions and answers about music and fashion, gossip and world events until the tea went cold.

Sabina fidgeted a little before saying, 'I'd like to instruct each of you separately sometimes, like we started doing in our previous lessons. That way you can each concentrate on the subjects that interest you most.'

'The herb-lore lessons we started were interesting,' Vreni said. She shrugged apologetically. 'But I don't seem to remember much from them at all.'

Sabina's eyes flicked around the room in an odd manner, and then she smiled. 'Don't be too hard on yourself,' she said finally. 'The Pratigs Māsa, the Wise Sisters, train for many years to develop their skills and knowledge. We have time enough for you to learn what you need to.'

'Learn what I need to? But I'm not one of the Sisters.'

'Well, think of it as a family tradition.' Sabina looked uneasy for a moment. 'In this technological world, they want us believe that the time of magic is in the past, but nature still has amazing resources to offer, if you learn how to use them.'

'But it's not just nature.' Vreni said. She felt that Sabina's answer was a bit shallow. 'What about the charm the Wise Sisters gave Papa? Surely magic that strong can't be brushed aside so casually. The power must still be there or Papa would be dead and gone by now, like Peters.' She pressed her lips together firmly.

If there was no magic, the curse would disappear and their family would be free. What was all this double talk about?

Vreni decided to play along with Sabina and her superficial answers. 'Of course I want to learn more about herbs.

Then maybe I can make a love potion and get a boyfriend, or make a charm to convince Papa to let us go somewhere.'

Sabina stood abruptly, looking serious. 'Vreni, it's herb lore for you, and for Rita, art and design I believe. But for now, history.'

Sabina had ignored her hint again. 'Sabina, could you plan a trip for us,' she said, 'to the city maybe? Somewhere that would help with our studies, of course.'

'We went to the zoo when we were younger,' Rita added, 'two tutors ago.'

'I'll give it some thought,' Sabina said.

Vreni sighed. Sabina had said that before and nothing had happened.

They settled themselves at a large round table in the centre of the conservatory where they spent several hours studying most days. Over the years they had studied languages, history, geography, mathematics, science, the arts and literature.

History and geography had always been the most interesting to Vreni. The world had changed so much over her own, century-long lifetime, and the stories in her family's journals wound back for hundreds of years. People and events from history intrigued her.

Sabina began as she always did, by retelling some version of the family history.

'Many centuries ago, before the cursing, your family traded within the Hanseatic League. They had developed strong skills for investment, so over the centuries their wealth grew enormously. This monetary power allowed us—you,' she corrected sharply, 'to pick and choose where and when to move, so the family stayed hidden from the world. The Baltic was the world back then, and it was so big that hiding was easy ...'

Vreni's thoughts drifted. *What would it have been like if the curse had never been put in place, or if it could have been removed somehow? But then she would have lived all her years back in a different time. She would never have seen all the changes throughout her century. Her family would have lived a different life, and she would never have been this Vreni, living in this time.*

Sabina coughed loudly and Vreni focused again.

'... the family was very influential, trading and travelling the rivers of Europe,' Sabina was saying. 'Then the cursing caused them to turn all of their endeavours inward, to protect and conceal their own, but their generosity had bred staunch loyalties and many people helped the family seep into the forests and take up a reclusive life.'

'But they had the magic,' Vreni challenged.

'They did,' Sabina agreed, 'but so did Veca Tante, and she was enraged when she heard that the Wise Sisters had softened the curse. She still wanted your grandmother Ieva dead, and if she couldn't do it with magic, then she, and her alchemists, would find a more direct way.'

'But when we sleep, aren't we —' Vreni's question trailed off.

'When you sleep, you don't age or die, but if you're harmed enough the injury becomes fatal when you wake,' Sabina said quietly.

'So they hid Grandmama Ieva from Veca Tante.'

Sabina nodded. 'There were other concerns, too. The Christians made pilgrimages into the northlands, and they wouldn't have taken lightly to meeting women who seemed to stay alive forever, nor would they have looked kindly on women with the unexplainable *powers* the Wise Sisters possessed. As the Son of God grew in importance, the word *witch* replaced the name Pratigs Māsa, or Wise Sisters. The family stayed hidden, and their caretakers became secretive although they remained loyal to them throughout the centuries.'

Vreni knew most of the family history, but each retelling added another layer.

'Over those earlier centuries people always desired to invade and control,' Sabina said, 'but in this last hundred years since you girls were born, there have been weapons and technologies that seem to have shrunk the world down to the size of a colourful toy ball.' Sabina held up Vreni's yarn ball and threw it toward her.

'Many nations have claimed the Baltic territories since your grandmother's time,' Sabina said, 'but there were still places to hide back then. When the Soviets swept in with cruel indifference and greed, seeking a coastal port that wouldn't freeze their ships in place in winter, they wanted everything. It seemed they could see everything, so the Wise Sisters and your family decided to hide in plain sight among the refugees fleeing the war, and we travelled to our new life, here.'

When the time had come to flee, Vreni and Rita had been in long-sleep, but everyone else was awake so the travel plans were finalised quickly, and they had walked away towards a new life. Parvils had called it luck that they were both asleep, because many border officials thought they were ill and hurried them through in case they caught the sickness.

Their father told them they were wonderful actresses, trying to make light of the huge changes, but at times Vreni still felt panic at the strangeness of having woken in this strange new place, with its topsy-turvy seasons, strange animals and plants, and everything she had known gone.

'Enough history for now,' Sabina said. 'Vreni, I'll work with you today. You can go, Rita, but no more shopping.'

Rita made a quick exit from the conservatory before Sabina could change her mind.

Vreni's stomach lurched as she remembered how dizzy and out of control she had felt after her last private lesson with Sabina.

Why can I only remember fragments of those other lessons? If it was some kind of family tradition, why wasn't Rita doing them too?

Signs and Secrets

*For the magic of the glimmer to continue to
hold strong, Veronika needs to freely agree
to the beginnings of her preparations. Invite
her to join us someday, and her acceptance
will add strength to the glimmer's spell.*

~ Instructions to Sister Sabina

'**Why** doesn't Rita get the same lessons as me?'

Sabina gathered her thoughts for longer than she usually did before she spoke. 'The Wise Sisters are your heritage, Vreni. The first of us were your grandmother's aunts, so it's in your blood, and we see potential in you.'

'For magic? But I—'

'The Wise Sisters employ many types of knowledge, and practise many skills to keep the old magic alive.'

'And you'll teach me? But why not Mama or her sisters? What about Rita?'

'We've watched all the sleepers and waited. We, the Wise Sisters, see in you the signs of something the others don't have. For reasons you will understand later, it has once more become important that the magic stays strong, and grows even stronger still. I—we—would like you to learn our ways so that one day you will add your strength to the Wise Sisters'.'

'Me, become a Wise Sister?'

'It will be your choice, one day. Can I ask you, out of tradition, not to share this conversation with anyone?' Sabina said.

'I-I won't,' Vreni stammered.

'Thank you, Vreni,' Sabina said. 'And now, enough of this chatter. For now, we'll continue with herb lore. Let's see ...' she said, thumbing through a thick notebook with a rich blue leather cover.

Vreni's head spun with the strange newness of what she had heard, with the idea that she might join Sabina and someday learn all about the magic and become—what?

'Sabina?'

'I know, you're full of questions.' Sabina closed the book and took Vreni's hands. 'I've been kind and cruel to you all at once, so I'll tell you just a little more about being a Wise Sister. There's a lot to learn, and you need patience and self-control, so start practising those right now,' Sabina said, smiling.

Vreni groaned as Sabina pointed to the blue book.

'You've been learning about using gems as charms for strength and protection ...'

Sabina's voice started to sound distant, full of echoes.

'... and how to use cloves to ...'

The words bounced in and around in Vreni's awareness. They were slippery. It was hard to hold their meaning.

The room became hazy around her. It tilted and seemed to lose its edges.

'... use your voice to release your intentions, to influence or enliven a spell ...'

Vreni heard many voices. She could feel her throat vibrate with song. Her ears throbbed; they were full of chanting. Was she a part of this music? She wasn't sure. Her heart beat in time to the strange phantom rhythm—she could feel swaying movement all around her—and then all was quiet again.

'... fragrances from herbs and oils can soothe, persuade, defend ...'

The air around Vreni was now a hazy tangle, thick with cloying aromas; her nose twitched as each new fragrance drifted past her, twisting on the meandering air. She breathed in the sweet vapours. Words, fragrances and images became a confusing broth in her mind.

'Liquorice brings new love and clove for compliance ... burdock and caraway will offer protection ... geranium is a healer ... courage from cardamom ... pine and sage for the sacred wisdom ... beech is wish magic ...'

Vreni became aware of the conservatory again.

'Well done, Vreni, that was a great afternoon's work,' Sabina said.

'Thank you.'

The lesson writhed and squirmed just out of reach of her memory. No matter how hard she tried to hold it clearly in her mind, it faded away, just as the others had before it, but she didn't tell Sabina. She didn't want her tutor to change her mind and think Vreni wasn't worthy of training as a Wise Sister.

—⁓—

The days and weeks after Vreni woke crawled by. Sabina came and went from the house. Vreni overheard more hushed arguments between her and Papa. They tried to make it look like Papa was walking her to her car, or helping her with a task, but the tension between them and their heated conversations were evident.

Vreni had asked Sabina again if she would take them on an outing, maybe to a natural history museum, or the botanical gardens. No plans were made.

The private lessons continued, and remained misty and confusing. Sabina assured Vreni that she was pleased with her progress, but Vreni felt increasingly confused and frustrated by her forgetfulness.

Between lessons there was time for music, books, the internet and the ponies, but even with all these distractions Vreni felt like a bird in a cage, unable to stretch her wings and fly.

Parvils had noticed her restlessness, and he was spending extra time with her, engaging her in long discussions. She loved debating with him; he had a knack of taking an opposing view in everything. But she didn't want to just observe the world, or debate about it; she wanted, desperately, to be part of it.

Yes, she had a history, a past, and a present that never changed, but she didn't seem to have a future—not one that she had chosen anyway.

When yet another day's lessons had finished, Vreni mumbled goodbye to Sabina and went to the tower to be alone.

The room at the top of the tower was an octagonal glass chamber ringed with low window seats. During the day it was flooded with light and the changing colours of the sky. At night, the glass became a strange kaleidoscope, reflecting and re-reflecting the room. Some nights she would turn off the lights and the room became an observatory, surrounded by the jewels of stars, and the creamy light of the moon.

At least up in the tower she could look out over the world and pretend she had a chance of being out there one day.

The sky was filling with angry clouds. She watched the sea turn from a calm sparkling blue into a thrashing hideous monster, rearing and howling as the storm winds came. She had a storm inside her too—twitchy, discouraged, fuming.

She flung open the windows and let the storm gust in and mix with her own angry tempest. Her tears mixed with the cold, stinging raindrops.

The storm passed. She tried to shake off her feelings of frustration as the afternoon sun broke through the thinning clouds. Standing in the centre of the tower room, she turned slowly, looking at the cliff edge and the sea, then the fruit trees and stables, next the pine grove to the west, with glimpses of the road beyond that led to the world.

She kept turning, her eyes skimming across the organised patchwork of the garden beds and back to the sea. Staring out the tower window at the calming waves, she waited for her composure to return.

Monsters

We never know when the sleep will call,
so birthdays make no sense at all.
Count the days you've been awake,
to know when it's time for gifts and cake.

~ Family rhyme

'**Looking** for sea monsters, Vreni?' Rita said as she appeared at the top of the tower stairs.

Vreni huffed out a weak laugh and turned toward her sister. 'Maybe we're the monsters now. Freaks.' She sighed and looked back at the sea.

'Come on, Vreni, think of all the things we've seen because of who we are,' Rita said, trying to lighten her sister's mood. 'What about cars, Vreni, *automobiles*? They're not as friendly as horses, but there are no droppings to pick up.'

Vreni smiled and sat on the narrow top step next to Rita. 'I remember how frightening cars seemed when I was young, but you held my hand and I felt safe,' Vreni said.

'Well, I was your big sister for a while back then, and that was my job,' Rita said.

'So many changes.'

'Electricity.' Rita nudged.

'Radio.' Vreni nudged back.

'Television.' Rita covered her face with her hands. 'I thought you'd captured fairies and put them in a strange glass cage for me.'

'Well, *I* was the big sister then.'

'I cried when Papa turned off the TV.' Rita laughed. 'I thought the fairies had died.'

'The moon landing!' Vreni grabbed Rita's hand. 'Rita, I wish you'd been awake in 1969; I watched as they landed on the moon. I couldn't breathe as Neil Armstrong stepped onto that new world. I thought that by now we'd *all* be able to go to the moon any time we liked.'

Rita laughed. 'Earth to Vreni! What about the dresses, shorter, and shorter, and shorter,' she said, pulling up her skirt.

'Jeans!' Vreni said. 'I could kiss the genius who invented jeans.'

'Neil Armstrong and the jeans genius—Vreni, I think you need a real boyfriend.' Rita ducked and laughed as Vreni swung to slap her.

'I wish,' Vreni said. 'Anyway, I've been looking through my journal and I counted my days awake. Since 1904, I've been awake for five thousand, eight hundred and thirty days. I'll be sixteen soon.'

'Me, too,' Rita said. 'I was born two years later, but I've counted five thousand, eight hundred and twenty-seven days awake, so we're twins now.' She laughed.

Vreni was enjoying listening to Rita buzzing with gossip and girl talk. They weren't often awake at the same time, so these moments together were a pleasure. Who else would understand her daydreams about boyfriends, or of spending time alone and out in the world, away from her family's always-watchful eyes.

'We have birthdays coming up,' Rita said, nudging her out of her daydream. 'Let's shop for presents. Thank goodness they invented the internet. How boring life was before online shopping.' Rita opened her laptop.

'But what about *real* shops?' Vreni said. 'Going to real shops, or out to eat lunch, or the cinema, or dancing, a party, an art gallery, a concert, maybe even travel. I want to be part of the world, Rita, not just watching it on that thing.' Vreni pointed to the laptop, its screen flickering with bright colours.

They planned a fantasy day of shopping in the city. Rita flicked from one website to another, all showing images of shops with their windows crammed with fashion, and streets crowded with people. Vreni imagined walking from shop to shop, surrounded by the excitement of the city, people everywhere, eating, talking, laughing, holding hands, sharing a kiss.

'How could we be almost sixteen and never have made any ordinary decisions on our own?' Vreni said. 'We've never even had to decide when it was it safe to cross the road.'

'Well, let's decide now. Come on, we'll make a list of birthday presents and order something special,' Rita said, shoving the computer into Vreni's lap.

'What I want, when I turn sixteen, is to be able to *act* like I'm sixteen. To go *there*,' she said, jabbing at the images on the screen, 'and not be trapped here, having the world delivered in postage bags.' She slammed the laptop closed.

'We could ask Papa if we could go to the shops instead of having presents delivered,' Rita said sceptically.

'I've already asked Sabina about a study trip and she acted like she'd never heard me, so I can't imagine how Papa would react if we asked.'

———

Vreni tried to forget about the city and concentrate on her studies, but one afternoon, during a private lesson with Sabina, she was distracted again by the idea.

'Vreni, you look troubled,' Sabina said.

Vreni sighed. *If anyone were going to be sympathetic, surely it would be Sabina.*

'I'm just restless,' she said. 'It's always lessons and crafts and amusements. I can't make you understand, because you're part of the world. You can't know how trapped I feel, and Papa seems satisfied to stay in his own private world, so how could I convince him? I want to go somewhere. I want to go to the city.'

'You've seen a lot of the world on the computer,' Sabina said gently. 'It's different for you girls now, and I can understand your feelings, but remember your unique situation.'

'I'm sure it *is* unique to be a prisoner in your own home,' Vreni said bitterly.

Sabina squeezed her hand.

'It's not like it was for Mama or Grandmama. Things are different now. Please, Sabina,' she whispered.

'Things are changing now,' Sabina said, more to herself than Vreni. 'I've been talking about such things with Parvils.'

'I've seen you and Papa together.' Vreni hesitated but continued. 'What are you two always arguing about?'

For a moment Sabina looked like she'd been caught out in a secret, and she looked down at the ground before answering. 'He's your father, so he's interested in ... how your lessons are progressing.'

'Papa could come and join in with the lessons anytime he wanted to,' challenged Vreni.

'He's protective of his daughters, of course. He isn't very happy with the interest we have in your future.'

'About me joining the Pratigs Māsa?'

'He has some reservations.'

'Why would he be worried? The Sisters have always protected us.'

'Well ...' Sabina looked at the floor.

What isn't she telling me?

'He's concerned about you having an outing.'

'So you're trying to arrange something.' Vreni heart galloped and she forgot her concerns.

'I have a few ideas in mind,' Sabina mumbled.

'Like what? The city?' Vreni squeezed Sabina's hands.

'I need to talk more with your father.'

—m—

There were more heated conversations between Sabina and Parvils over the next few days. Vreni could never hear what was being said. She hoped the debate was about the trip to the city. She thought she would feel better if she told Rita about her conversation with Sabina, but after she did, she had to listen to Rita's endless chattering what-ifs, which seemed to double the agony of waiting for Papa's answer.

Fledglings

I know Parvils has been reluctant, but the world has changed too much, and secluding the sleepers is not a viable strategy with this generation, or for our plans to free the family from the curse. Arrange an outing, but plan it well. We need to see what our bird is like when she leaves her cage; we may need her to work with us very soon.

~ Sister Anna's counsel to Sister Sabina and Parvils

'**I've** been talking with Sabina about an outing,' Papa said, sipping his coffee.

'Finally,' Vreni whispered. She squeezed Rita's hand under the table.

'Most fathers don't wait a century before their daughters come to them seeking permission or his blessing to venture out into the world.'

'Well, Papa, surely you don't mean to keep us prisoner here forever,' Vreni said jokingly.

'All this was so much easier in the old times,' Papa said. 'Back then there were so many rules about what a young woman couldn't do that a father didn't have to be the one saying no. The whole of society said it for him.'

Parvils toyed with the magical amulet hanging around his neck as he looked at his daughters, who seemed restless and determined. He had listened to Sabina talking about her plans for Vreni's training. Even though he was concerned, he was not in any position to resist the guidance of the Wise Sisters, so he had agreed.

Parvils smiled at Vreni. He had known many years of waiting, so he understood her restlessness too well. Rita was a squirrel out to gather pretty things, but Vreni was a bird that was becoming too big for the nest. He knew she needed to spread her wings and fly, even just for a short while. This moment was always going to come: the moment when his daughters would seek a world bigger than family and home.

'When I met your mother back in 1867, just having a husband was adventure enough for her.' He smiled. 'But things have changed. You've seen glimpses of what you're missing. This internet is a bad thing for fathers because it shows you the world. But how can I stop my fledglings from wanting to fly away from the nest?'

'So we can go?' Vreni held her breath.

'Yes, you can go, but there are rules,' he cautioned, 'lots of rules.'

'Thank you, Papa,' the sisters said in unison. They hugged their father, spilling his coffee.

'I'll be in danger if your mother wakes while you're away in the city shopping.' He smiled, mopping up the mess.

'Uncle Artūrs will drive you into the city and stay outside every shop at all times.'

'Of course, Papa,' Rita said.

'Whatever you think best,' Vreni said.

Artūrs was her father's trusted companion, and the protector of his most precious things. Vreni knew that without Artūrs watching over their every move, there would be no shopping trip. She told herself it would be enough freedom—for now.

Shop Till You Drop

*Archangel root and thistle to safeguard
against danger, sage for wisdom, cardamom
for courage, clove and a grain of liquorice
for friendship, and garnet for protection.*

~ Vreni's glimmer journal

Vreni woke early, too excited to sleep. *The city.* The words rang in her ears. 'The amazing, mysterious, exciting city,' she whispered. She imagined wings unfurling as she stretched.

She may have travelled halfway around the world with her family, but she had never even bought herself a coffee on her own. Now finally Papa was allowing them to go to the city and she had her chance for a little freedom.

She quickly washed her face and bundled her hair into a knot on top of her head, then rifled excitedly through the decades within her closet, choosing boots, her favourite washed-out jeans, T-shirt, scarf. As she pulled on her jacket she smiled at her memories of the strange things women had considered fashionable throughout her century, and what might come next.

She checked herself quickly in the mirror, grabbed her bag and hurried to Rita's room, thumping on the door.

'Shop till you drop, sister,' she called.

'I'm way ahead of you,' Rita called from halfway down the curving stairs.

Vreni chased after her and they burst into the kitchen together.

'I fear for the family fortune, letting you two modern young ladies loose near real shops,' Parvils said. 'I've seen the accounts from your spending through that awful device.' He passed over two steaming bowls of porridge.

'Online shopping, Papa,' Rita said, trying to convince her father of the virtues of the computer as they ate. 'It brings us amazing things from far away, just like the travelling traders who used to call in the summers in Vārve.'

'But back in Vārve,' Parvils said, 'I got to decide which traders to turn away from the door, or at least I could strike a bargain. Sometimes poor Artūrs can barely carry all your parcels from the post office. Be kind to him on your trip today, and make sure you leave something for other people to buy.'

Parvils smiled as he watched his daughters eating breakfast, chirping excitedly about their adventure like a pair of baby birds.

The car ride to the city only took an hour, but to Vreni, fidgeting in the back seat, it felt far longer. As they drove through the deserted coastal scrublands towards the edges of the city suburbs, she pinched herself once or twice to check she wasn't dreaming; it all felt as though it might be magic. She thought about what Sabina could have said to make Papa agree. Maybe she *had* used magic.

She was wondering more and more about magic, especially when she thought about the strange private lessons she was having. There were no secrets in the family about things like the Pratigs Māsa softening the curse, or Papa's long-life charm, but apart from that her family didn't feel magical, and neither did her life, but the lessons were strange.

When would the Wise Sisters ask her to join them? She was finding it so difficult to remember the lessons that maybe she wouldn't be good enough after all.

Vreni shivered and turned her attention to her sister. 'Do you know what you're going to buy?' she asked Rita.

'Shoes are the hardest thing to buy online,' Rita said, sounding like an expert. 'I've bought so many pairs and returned nearly all of them.' She rolled her eyes at Artūrs as he groaned from the driver's seat.

'I'm too busy for shoes,' Artūrs said, smiling over his shoulder. 'And the postmistress winks at me now when I say hello.'

'Don't worry, Uncle Artūrs, I'll try on every pair of shoes I can to save you from the postmistress,' Rita said.

'Shoes would be nice,' Vreni agreed. She flicked the corners of a thin bundle of money, and then shoved it back in her pocket. 'But not those heels you wear, they look dangerous. All the colours are so bright now that it'll be hard to choose but definitely a red pair and maybe—'

'We don't have to choose,' Rita said, as she waved a small plastic card in the air between them. 'We have cash and this card. Do you remember the *PIN*?'

'Of course I do,' Vreni said.

Rita laughed. 'It'll be like we have Papa with his pockets full of money right beside us in every shop.'

'I saw some beautiful chains on TV, very long silver chains with amazing charms on them, and necklaces made of crystals,' Vreni said. 'I want to go to jewellery shops to look at all that sparkling stuff.'

'Bling.'

'Bling?'

'Bling,' Rita said knowledgably. 'Accessories.'

Vreni nodded and shrugged. 'I'd love a scarf.'

'*Another* scarf?' Rita tugged on the scarf around Vreni's neck. 'Don't you already have seventy-five?'

'And don't you already have enough shoes?'

When their list was complete they became quiet, with nothing left to do but stare out the car windows, watching the sea of houses crushing more closely together, and the roads becoming wider and busier.

The buildings of the approaching city loomed high into the sky. Vreni's heart was fluttering at the thought of even this small amount of freedom.

—❦—

Vreni was used to the space of home. The city was like a dense forest of buildings, sprouting lights and signs. It expanded until it was almost too large for her to comprehend. The computer had shown her city scenes and she had felt eager to be part of it, but now that she was here everything seemed so frantic. Crowds of people raced up and down the sidewalks, and darted in front of the car in such a hurry.

She flopped back onto the seat and stared out at the sky for a moment. She opened the car window and her ears filled with roaring engines and honking horns. Clanking, disharmonious music was blaring from a group busking outside a crowded cafe. The air had a gritty feel, and smelled of dust and exhaust fumes. But drifting over it came the delightful aroma of freshly baked pastries, and the sweet fragrance of a flower shop with buckets of blossoms spilling into the street.

Everything was so fast and so loud; she felt the energy of the city all around her.

Artūrs manoeuvred the car through the traffic while the girls gave him directions from Vreni's phone. Vreni liked the phone more than the computer; it felt like a symbol of her independence. After finding a place to park, Artūrs told them he would wait for them and then take them to the next place they wanted to go.

Vreni glanced at Artūrs. Today he was Papa's most trusted eyes and ears, and their protector. People like Artūrs had served with love and loyalty through the centuries following the cursing, but Artūrs seemed the closest and most loyal of all.

Vreni wondered again about magic. Did Artūrs give his loyalty freely?

The question vaporised as Rita opened the car door and pulled Vreni by the arm onto the bustling foot path and into the first shop.

—⁂—

By the end of the morning's shopping they had almost filled the car with purchases. Vreni's confidence was growing with every hour they spent in the city.

Artūrs insisted that he would not eat burgers and fries for anyone, so they conceded and let him choose a more stylish restaurant where they could buy food more like the type of midday meal he favoured: something heavy, spicy, and piled generously on a large plate.

After lunch the shopping continued. The girls' goal was to visit every shop on their list. Sometimes they bought things, but often they just looked and talked to all the people they met, soaking up the hype of the city.

—⁂—

The very last of the day's light flowed crimson-orange between the city buildings. Shop lights were starting to glow. When the sun had almost set and the long summer day was melting into a warm evening, they persuaded Artūrs to let them stay in the city into the evening, for as long as the late trading lasted.

Artūrs was happy to accommodate them. He had enjoyed an easy day of reading and napping, and the temptation of choosing another restaurant for dinner before they returned home was all the encouragement he needed.

The girls entered a store called Thing. On the back wall was a huge screen showing music clips, with people dancing in a sea of brilliant strobing colour. The music washed over Vreni as she and Rita danced in and out of the racks of clothes and accessories, holding up outfits.

'The purple or the green?' Rita called, doing a quick turn to show off a top, with a second one draped over her shoulder.

'Green.' Vreni danced past with an armful of clothes, blowing a kiss as she went into the changing room.

As Rita returned the purple top to the display, she saw a man walk into the shop and move over to a wall covered with posters for concerts and dance parties.

'So, do I look like a gypsy now?' Vreni said, coming out of the changing room.

She saw the man near Rita, and watched him for a moment, gathering details in a series of glances. *Tall, spikey fair hair, nice broad shoulders ...* She smiled at herself and her thoughts, and breathed out slowly.

He looked toward her, but when she caught his eye he quickly looked at the wall again. He wore a long brown coat, which hung down to his calves. The coat lay open, showing a white T-shirt with the word *PARADOX* printed on the front in orange lettering.

Vreni could not look away. His eyes were a piercing blue-grey, like a stormy sky.

He looked towards her again, and smiled. 'Well, I don't think you look like a gypsy,' he said. He held her in his gaze as he walked toward her. 'Hi, I'm William, gypsy fashion expert, at your service.' He offered his hand, and his smile broadened.

'I'm Vreni, absolutely not a gypsy.' She shook his hand, and her breath caught in her throat. 'This is my sister Rita.'

'Are the new clothes for tonight?' He pointed at a dance-party poster on the overcrowded wall. 'If you're going, maybe we could get some food before it starts. It's only five blocks east of here and the night markets are on, so we could look around there and eat.'

William still held Vreni's hand. Her heart was thumping. She stood frozen, caught up in his smiling gaze, not wanting him to let go. She could hear lots of good advice circling on the edges of her thoughts—advice about making sensible decisions—but she decided instead to go with her impulse.

'Yes, we'll be there tonight,' she said, her mind racing. 'We have a few things to do on the way, but I promise you a dance.' *What am I doing? But I might never get a chance like this again.*

Rita squeezed her arm, hard, but Vreni ignored her.

'Just one dance? But I've got some stylish moves,' he said comically, still staring at Vreni. 'See you tonight.' He lifted the hand he was still holding and kissed it lightly, then turned and left the shop.

Vreni looked at her freshly kissed hand; it was trembling.

'What is your problem?' Rita said, punching Vreni's arm hard. 'How can we go to that dance party? Have you found some spell to send Papa to sleep, and Uncle Artūrs as well?'

Vreni felt as though she was being squeezed. She saw this as a single chance to escape the cage she had been held in until today.

'What, so you're telling me that lessons with Sabina and endless shopping is enough for you?' she snapped. 'Well, your carriage awaits.' She jabbed a finger toward the window, where they could see their uncle dozing in the parked car in the dim evening light.

Vreni walked over to the sales assistant and paid for the new clothes they were wearing. 'Is there a back door from the shop we could use?' she asked the shop assistant.

'Sure, through there.' The woman pointed, only half paying attention.

Vreni checked the address and time on the poster and stuffed her old clothes into her bag. 'Tonight, sister, we will *not* be sleeping princesses.'

She eased open the shop's back door and stepped, determined, into the alleyway. She stood holding her breath until she heard Rita grumble and slam the door behind her.

Dance Party

The girls stood close to each other for a few moments in the gloom of the alley.

'You've lost your mind, Vreni,' Rita snapped.

'Maybe I've lost my mind, but I've still got my brave sister.' Vreni looked at Rita. 'We have this chance, Rita, to be normal, to do things other girls take for granted.' She pecked Rita's cheek to lighten the mood. 'Anyway, we have some money, a mobile phone, and brave Uncle Artūrs to rescue us when we're tired of dancing with handsome guys.'

'And Papa?' Rita asked.

'Just a few hours of living, real living, and we'll return to our jail.'

'Jail?'

'Come on, Rita,' she said, grabbing her sister's arm.

They moved to the end of the alley and stopped. All at once Vreni felt very alone. Her hands were suddenly clammy. She wiped them on her jeans and turned east, following the people that she guessed were moving towards the night markets.

The evening streets became more noisy and congested as they walked. Crowds were gathering in the vibrant market square that had been set up in a blocked-off street, and stood about, clogging the footpaths, talking and listening to music. People were clustered around stalls and food vendors. Tables and chairs caused lumpy blockages outside restaurants, and spicy aromas filled the evening air.

Vreni led the way through the confusion of sensations, pushing through the frantic joy of it all. They stopped at stalls selling trinkets that Rita had called bling. Vreni found a new scarf, made of silk and bordered with lace and fringing.

Rita pointed. 'Look at her.'

A street performer was standing frozen like a statue while people tried to distract her and make her move. The audience rewarded her skills by throwing money into a wooden box at her feet.

Rita laughed. 'You could stand me here next time I'm in long-sleep and I'd earn us thousands.'

'Then you could buy even more shoes,' Vreni joked.

An acrid, chemical odour caught Vreni's attention. She heard a strange noise behind her, and saw the crowd disappearing out of the corner of her eye. She braced herself for trouble. She grabbed Rita protectively and turned them around.

The crowd had formed around a wide space, and in the centre of the circle were two shirtless men spinning flaming metal staffs around their heads and throwing them into the air across the circle to each other. A few people carrying drums pushed through the crowd. The first drummer offered a rhythm and the rest joined in, laying down a frenzied fast–slow of pulsing beats as if they were one mind, or one raucous beating heart.

The fire twirlers were now moving in time to the beat. Two girls joined the fire-dance, spinning burning balls of flames on the end of a glinting silver chain. The moving flames painted arcs of orange on the night sky.

The glorious noise and the dancing flames filled Vreni's awareness. Her heart took up the beat and calmed the racing nervousness she had felt ever since leaving the shop.

The two girls bounced through the street market until they became aware of their hunger. They found a sparse, brightly lit cafe filled with battered old tables and chairs that were unoccupied.

Vreni nudged her sister. 'We can have the burgers we missed out on at lunch.'

'Hello, beauties,' said a crumpled old woman sitting behind the counter. 'What will you have?'

'Burgers?' Vreni realised she wasn't sure how to order. 'And coffee with milk, thank you.' When the crumpled woman had written down their order and shuffled off to the kitchen, she said, 'Pick a table Rita.'

'Do you think Uncle Artūrs has told Papa yet?'

Vreni's stomach clenched. She smiled and shrugged, not mentioning the times her phone had vibrated in her pocket over the last couple of hours. 'The dance party will be starting soon. I have to see it, but then we'll call Uncle Artūrs straight away, okay?' she said, trying to sound reassuring.

The burgers arrived, but they ate half-heartedly, their stomachs too tight for more than a few mouthfuls. Soon they abandoned their meal and left the quiet cafe. Vreni found the warehouse on her phone and they zigzagged the last block and a half east.

The aging warehouse, now a dance club, glowed in a storm of flashing colour. The whole building pulsated with sound, sending waves of vibration through the streets. Vreni felt her heart change its rhythm to match the beat of the music.

'Vreni! Rita!'

William waved from beside the front door. He jumped between them and wrapped an arm around each of them as though they were old friends. Vreni also received an unexpected kiss on her cheek, causing her heart to rebel against the rhythm of the music.

Kiss, her mind sang, *kiss, kiss, kiss.*

William gave a friendly nod to the man at the door, who nodded back and waved them into the dark musty shadows of the foyer.

'William.' Vreni finally found her voice as they walked toward the door. 'You really wanted your dance, then?'

'Still just one dance?' William said, leading the girls inside. 'Very funny.'

They stepped through the door and the music hammered at Vreni's ears. The massive vaulted space was a jungle of light that flashed and twisted as if it was alive. People danced in and out of the light, appearing and disappearing from view. Friends were clustered together on the edges of the dance floor, or at small tables, smiling and laughing, and trying to hear each other talking.

Vreni noticed couples in the shadowy places away from the crowd, enjoying a space all their own. Vreni thought of William's kiss, and her cheek felt hot.

'I'll find us a table,' William said. 'Do you want me to take that so you can dance?'

Vreni patted her pockets to make sure she had the phone, cash and card, then eased her backpack from her shoulder and handed it to William.

The girls took excited, unsure steps out onto the dance floor. For Vreni, it was amazing to be surrounded by the music, feeling the rhythm pulsing deep into her bones. No matter how loud they turned up the music when they danced up in their tower, it didn't compare to the energy of sharing this experience with a crowd. The thrill she felt pushed away any last morsel of nervousness she had.

Moving in and around the sea of dancing bodies, she noticed the looks some of the guys in the crowd were giving them.

It felt strange. Vreni knew she was blushing. She felt flattered, and returned some of the looks with smiles.

She grabbed Rita, and moved to join a large crowd of girls who were laughing and dancing with their hands up in the air. The girls welcomed them, and they all bumped happily into each other as they danced. Vreni could smell all the different perfumes as she moved closer to the dancers. The feeling of belonging was delightful.

William's face appeared within the circle and he danced towards Vreni. He moved in close to her and took her hands. Her heart became acrobatic. He continued dancing, moving her backward until they had left the crowd of dancing girls behind.

Looking over William's shoulder, Vreni saw Rita laughing and pointing at her, kissing the air, before smiling and turning back to the circle of happy dancers.

William danced close to Vreni; they made their own private circle. People moved around them, and the lights flashed and the music throbbed, but it all seemed to fade around Vreni until all she could see was William's face. She felt him close to her. It was dreamlike, but when she reached out to touch him, he *was* real and right there.

He wrapped his arms around her waist, leaned in and kissed her lightly. She felt giddy, amazed by everything that had happened; her absolute joy at being free and normal, and the kiss.

'You're wonderful,' she yelled.

He kissed her again.

Rita danced in between them and leaned in close. 'Three songs,' she said to Vreni, laughing. 'Enough dancing and definitely too much kissing.'

William winked, pointed to a table and walked over to it.

Vreni danced close to Rita and hugged her tight. 'This is all amazing.'

'Thank you, Vreni,' Rita said, ' for being brave and bringing me here.'

'It was nothing, just a small adventure for two sisters.' Then Vreni added, more seriously, 'I'll tell Papa it was all my idea.' She pointed across the dance floor. 'Little girl's room.'

Rita nodded and danced away towards William at the table.

—m—

Vreni stood for a moment in the gloom of the narrow hallway, giving her eyes time to adjust after leaving the bright lights of the toilets. An arm reached across her shoulders and she turned, expecting to see William next to her, but it was one of the many male faces that had ogled her on the dance floor. She smiled, moving away.

The man grabbed her and pulled her further down the dark hallway. She tried to cry out, but he pushed her against the wall and the air was squeezed out of her lungs, leaving her gasping. She pushed back against him, trying to free herself, but his broad body seemed to surround her.

'I've been watching you dancing.' His words felt sticky and hot against her neck. 'I like your moves,' he said in a whispered growl.

She drew in a ragged breath. Her blood burned with a flood of adrenaline. Then her fear suddenly boiled away, leaving anger in its place. *Well, how do you like this move?* Leaning her head to the side and bracing herself, she smacked her head into his temple.

The surprise of the unexpected headbutt earned her a moment, and she tried to free herself, but he grabbed her again, rougher now, and pressed his body hard up against her. Her lungs seemed frozen with returning fear. When she had gathered enough breath, she screamed.

He responded by shoving her. Her head hit the wall. She felt dizzy. She swallowed down the vomit rising in her throat. He leaned into her again. Then the heavy, stinking presence of the stranger was gone.

She felt light. *Am I dead?* Her body crumpled to the floor.

When she opened her eyes she saw William slamming her attacker against the opposite wall, then he lifted his knee with surprising force into the man's groin, causing him to collapse onto the floor and vomit violently on the carpet.

William scooped Vreni up into his arms. 'You're safe now, you're safe. It's all right.'

She sobbed like a frightened child, gulping air. She'd thought long-sleep was the worst fate she had to face, but now she realised there were many more curses in this world. William's arms felt like a place of refuge.

Two large uniformed men grabbed the vomit-covered menace. Taking an arm each, they dragged him towards the front door. Some of the dancers offered up mock cheers as he was delivered to the police.

William got a glass of water from the bar and offered it to Vreni, and they slowly returned to their table. Rita was sitting with her head leaning into the corner, her eyes closed.

Vreni sat down heavily and let William's arms surround her. She sipped the water slowly, and with each sip her mind began to clear. She looked at her watch. She would need to face her father soon. At least Papa's wrath would never seem as frightening, ever again, after what had just happened. She sighed deeply, shuddering.

'Thank you, William,' she said. 'I don't want to think about what might've happened if you hadn't been there.' She felt the tears welling in her eyes again.

'But I was there. Don't let some weird creep like that stop you from dancing.' He smiled, trying to lighten the mood. 'Or I won't get to dance with you anymore.'

Vreni thought about how wonderful the night had been, dancing with William, kissing him. She let herself imagine, for a fleeting second, that her life was somehow different. She pretended that a night like this one could happen again. But the weight of the curse fractured the brief dream.

'I'll give you my email address,' William said.

'Great,' she said, knowing she would probably never use it but wishing she could somehow see him again.

She could imagine William being part of her life, the way her father was part of her mother's life, watching and waiting while she slept. But reality intruded. How could she do that to someone? How could she begin to explain to William what her life was like?

'Rita, come on, it's time to go,' she said, nudging her sister. Rita didn't move.

'Wow, she's a sound sleeper. I can't imagine nodding off in here.' William looked around the chaotic dance space.

Vreni's mind froze on one thought. *Sleep. Rita was asleep.*

'Wake up, Rita, we've got to go home.' Vreni shook her sister wildly. 'No! Not here, not now. Please, wake up.'

If I Die Before I Wake

*The body of a sleeper undergoes total
cellular cessation during long-sleep. It does
not decompose; it will not heal. Whatever
happens to the body while in long-sleep
will take effect once the sleeper wakes.*

~ Pratigs Māsa, *New Records*

'What do you think she took?' William asked.

'What?' Vreni wheezed.

'You know, maybe she took a pill or something. You can get anything in a place like this.'

'No, not Rita, never.'

'Maybe someone slipped her something.'

'What? I need to call our—driver.' Vreni reached for the phone in her back pocket. The screen was smashed.

'Use mine.' William handed her his phone.

'I don't know the number. I've never had to call before.' Vreni felt like a child.

'No problem, my car's up the road,' William said.

He scooped Rita up into his arms and leaned in close to her face. Then he looked at Vreni with a strange expression.

He turned and raced around the edge of the dance floor to where the security guard stood near the entrance.

Vreni grabbed her bag and scrambled after him.

'Call an ambulance,' William was saying to the man, 'I think she's overdosed.'

He lay Rita on the matted shagpile carpet in the foyer and checked her pulse, then her breathing. Then he locked eyes with the guard on the phone and indicated 'hurry up' with a rapid circling of his index finger. He turned back to the lifeless Rita, checked her breathing and pulse once more, and started to give chest compressions.

'No!' Vreni screamed and threw herself over Rita's sleeping body. 'You can't do that.'

This is all so totally wrong. Rita should be hidden away by now. Vreni knew that Rita looked dead. All victims of the curse always appeared dead when they were in long-sleep. She whispered the words from the ancient tale. 'No breath or warmth or flutter of heart.'

'What?'

'Just get us out of here, please. Take us to your car. She'll be fine. I've seen this happen before,' Vreni begged. 'Please, now!'

'She won't be fine, Vreni. Let me help her ...'

The rest of William's words were drowned out by the sound of a siren; moments later two paramedics burst into the foyer.

'I think she's overdosed,' William said, stepping out of the way.

The paramedics closed in on Rita. Their presence stripped Vreni of any remnants of control she might have had over the situation.

'Just leave her alone,' Vreni screamed.

William placed his arms around her, but now they felt more like a trap than a refuge.

'Help me, William. Don't let them take her. They'll hurt her.'

On the stretcher, Rita was disappearing into the cool neon evening outside the club. The paramedics slid her into the back of the ambulance.

'No!' Vreni howled again, jumping in after them, staying close to her sister.

When William tried to follow, one of the paramedics stopped him, saying, 'Family only.' William showed the man a small card, which Vreni couldn't read, and sat down beside her as the ambulance doors slammed shut.

The smell of antiseptic and adrenalin in the cramped space was almost suffocating. Bright lights and the buzz of urgent conversation mixed with the endless screech of the siren. Vreni sat frozen, trapped in the unreality of it all. She could hear William talking to the paramedic, but the words held no meaning for her numb mind. All she could see was Rita's shiny pink stiletto heels and the tangles of her copper hair; everything else that was happening was hidden behind the hunched paramedic.

Vreni heard a ragged sigh escape William's chest. She saw the paramedic sag as though he'd been deflated, and then he leaned over and signalled the driver. The siren fell silent. The paramedic looked at William, who looked back knowingly.

'There was nothing they could do, Vreni. I'm so sorry.' William squeezed her hand tightly and leaned back against the side of the ambulance.

'I know,' she said, with a detachment she hoped would be taken for shock and disbelief.

What was I thinking? Why did I ever believe we could be part of the real world? She stared at Rita, feeling as small and fragile as a glass bird. *I have to fix this.*

'What will happen now?' Vreni needed information so she could try to form some kind of plan. She had to get Rita home, hidden and safe, or her foolishness would cost her family dearly.

'We'll need to tell your family,' William began gently. 'There'll be paperwork. They have to find out why she died, so they'll have to do an autopsy.' William looked at the paramedic, who nodded confirmation.

'Autopsy?' Vreni's mind came suddenly alert. Sleepers are suspended somewhere outside of time, but if something happens while they sleep, the harm simply waits until they wake. Rita would never survive having her body opened and pieces removed for examination.

'That can't happen,' she said, 'I need to get her home.'

Trust

William and Vreni followed as the paramedics wheeled the gurney carrying Rita through the emergency department doors. The surreal parade moved down the noisy corridor and stopped at a small, brightly lit cubicle.

Vreni stood close to Rita, brushing wisps of hair from her face.

'Vreni, she's gone,' William said.

'Just for now,' she answered. 'But if I don't get her home soon she may be gone forever. William, *please*.' She gripped his shoulder and whispered urgently into his ear. 'I would offer my own life to keep my sister safe. We—*I* need you to help me get her home. Then you'll understand everything.'

William hugged Vreni. He noticed her perfume. He breathed deeply and considered her request. Then he walked over and spoke quietly to the orderly, who turned and left them alone in the small white cubicle.

'We're lucky, I know the layout here.' He held out his ID card: *William Masters UNL*. 'I've been doing some lab stuff at this hospital for uni. My father is obsessed that I study science—whatever, the details can wait until later.'

'So you'll help us?'

'Somehow I do believe you, but now you need to trust me. In a moment we're going to leave Rita here and walk out.'

'But—'Her eyes stung.

'Trust.'

They walked out of Rita's cubicle and down the corridor past the triage desk, towards the exit. Vreni's feet felt like lead. William waved as they passed the desk. The staff looked at Vreni, then quickly looked away.

As they approached the main doors Vreni resisted the urge to run back to her sister. William took her arm and pushed her around the corner into a darkened corridor, and led the way towards the rear of the emergency rooms.

They re-entered Rita's cubicle. William quickly lifted up her limp body and they retreated into the half-lit hallway, hiding for a moment behind a storage cabinet before quietly moving back along the corridor. William looked from the main door to the fire door. Vreni wondered how they would get outside without being seen by the staff or setting off the fire alarm.

They stood in the shadows for long, agonising seconds. Vreni's heart thumped in her ears.

There were angry shouts as a scuffle broke out between two drunks in the waiting area. With all eyes focused on the fight, they took their chance and slipped out the main door and into the cool evening air.

'Help me with her,' William said. They each took one of Rita's arms and held her sagging body upright. 'Now she just looks like she's been drinking too much,' he said.

They walked as fast as they could with her dead weight between them. After a couple of blocks William veered into the same stark cafe Vreni and Rita had stopped in for dinner. The air inside the cafe was now thick with the rich aroma of roasted coffee and cinnamon.

They eased Rita into a booth. Her head lolled against the wall.

'Coffee, please,' William said to the crumpled woman who was reading a newspaper at the counter.

'Big party night, eh,' she grunted, nodding towards Rita.

'Yeah, but she'll be no trouble,' Vreni said.

The old woman served a steaming pot of coffee, and a smaller jug full of warmed milk. She flicked a strange glance at Rita and placed three cups on the table.

'She might smell my coffee and wake up,' the old woman said. Then she turned and shuffled back to her newspaper.

William poured a cup of coffee and gulped down a large mouthful. 'My car is maybe three blocks from here.'

'But—'

'Trust. I'll be back in ten minutes.' He pushed through the door and disappeared down the street, his long coat flapping as he ran.

Vreni poured a cup of milky coffee and watched as the old woman flicked slowly through her newspaper. People trailed in and out of the cafe. Vreni forced herself to sip at her coffee. She counted the sips and watched the clock. Twenty-seven sips and she'd finished her coffee. No William. She added milk to his half-finished cup.

Fourteen sips later headlights flared outside. William walked in the door and Vreni let herself take a deep breath. They eased Rita from the booth and headed for the door.

'You take Sleeping Beauty home, eh,' said the crumpled woman. She looked up from her paper and caught Vreni in her gentle stare. Vreni shivered as she felt the woman's gaze remain on her as they left the cafe.

With an effort, they manoeuvred Rita safely into the back seat of William's car.

'South,' Vreni said, slipping into the front seat.

William looked at her and then at Rita's reflection in the mirror. 'What the hell have I done?' he whispered. 'They'll know it was us. They know me at St Mark's. I spend time in the labs for uni, and my dad's corporation gives heaps of cash for research so they'll remember I was there for sure.'

He looked at Vreni, who hadn't heard anything he'd said. She was staring straight ahead into the night.

'Trust,' he whispered and headed for the motorway.

William

The young man is unaware of his lineage, but because of it, he can be instrumental to our cause. It's also useful that he's highly susceptible to the subtleties of herb and fragrance. Of course we cannot make him act against his will. We're fortunate that his unconscious desires align with our goals of attaining the potion. We must thank the fates for sending him to us.
~ Discussion between Sister Anna and Sister Sabina

Once in the car, Vreni spoke only to give William directions.

During the ten minutes since they had turned east off the highway William had been watching the set of headlights following in the rear-vision mirror. 'I didn't think we'd see anybody out here tonight.' He pointed over his shoulder.

Vreni turned her head quickly and looked. 'How long have they been behind us?'

'Not long,' answered William. 'Do you know who it is?'

'I think it's our driver, Artūrs.'

'How would he have found you?'

'Lucky coincidence?'

An image of the old woman from the cafe flashed into Vreni's mind. She could only speculate on how Artūrs had known they were heading towards home. She hadn't thought about what precautions he, Papa or the Sisters would have put in place to keep them safe.

A sudden flood of paranoia swept her. *How far would her family go to protect them? What were they capable of?* Suddenly feeling hot, she opened her window. The salty freshness of the sea air was cool on her face.

She knew things would never be the same again after this, but right now she didn't want to share any more weirdness with William. He was going to learn about her family soon enough.

The road became narrower and darker as they drove closer to home. Vreni watched William's face in the glow of the dash lights. The whole day was starting to feel fictional and far away. She reached out and touched his hand. He twined his fingers through hers and they drove down the narrow, dark road without speaking.

They rolled slowly up the gravel drive and pulled up in front of the house. Vreni saw her father waiting at the front door. He took a step towards them, but then he slowed and froze.

The dark blue Mercedes pulled up close, too close, behind them. Papa's face was stony. He opened his mouth to speak but the words seemed stolen.

Artūrs broke the silence. 'Parvils, they're safe,' he said, getting out of the Mercedes. 'Rita is—*sleeping*. This young man has brought them back to us safely.'

Vreni couldn't bear seeing the look on her father's face. She pushed open the car door and ran to him. 'Papa, I'm so sorry. I encouraged Rita to go on this foolish adventure with me. It was just meant to be an hour of dancing. My phone broke and I couldn't call when I needed to.'

'My daughters are safe,' Parvils managed to say with a forced, faraway voice, taking Vreni in his arms. 'It seems a new chapter is opened.' He nodded at William across the roof of the car.

William could only nod in response. He lifted Rita from the back seat and stood in the darkness waiting.

'Follow me.' Artūrs led him up the stone stairs and through the wide front door.

Vreni watched as her father took third place in the procession. She tried to speak again, but her words were trapped in her throat. What could she say to make the situation better? Who else would now know about their family and its secrets? Papa, Artūrs and many others had worked so hard to keep the family safe, and she couldn't even resist the impulse to run off and go dancing.

She wished she could travel back to the beginning of the day and do things differently so her father could now see her as a young woman and not a childish spoilt girl. She swallowed the sob rising in her throat and fell into line behind her father.

Artūrs led William up the curving stairs and along the carpeted landing towards Rita's room. Her eyes stayed on William's back as he carried his burden. As he turned a corner, Vreni saw him look through the open door of a softly lit room. On the bed inside was her sleeping mother. Her mama had slept for so long now that Vreni could not remember when she had last been awake.

She felt flushed with guilt. She couldn't even remember when she and her mother had last talked. *All I've worried about is my own selfish wishes.*

William's eyes locked on Gaida's sleeping form and his chest heaved. Then he looked down at Rita, and finally turned back to Vreni with a look that was full of questions.

They entered Rita's bedroom, which felt cramped to Vreni with so many people standing in the girlishly lavish space. William laid Rita gently on the bed. *What happens to William now?*

'I must thank you properly for protecting my daughters the way you did,' Papa said to William. His words were strong and gracious again. 'Let's sit in the library for a while, and enjoy some food, a drink.'

As the men left the room, Vreni finally let her bubbling emotions surface. Fear mixed with excitement, and guilt with pride. The feelings weighed heavily, and she sagged and sat next to her sleeping sister.

'Rita, I'm so sorry, I just meant to have a small adventure.' A slow tear rolled down Vreni's cheek. 'I never thought you would fall asleep. I should have stayed with you. No, I never should have made you go with me.'

Suddenly she was sobbing, and her words spilled out. 'You didn't see, but there was this horrible guy outside the toilets. He grabbed me. He wouldn't let me go. I was so scared I couldn't breathe.' Her tears splashed onto Rita's face. She wished the tears would wake her sister so she could be comforted. She curled up on the bed next to Rita, pressing her face into her sister's shoulder, and wept.

But Vreni had cried on sleeping shoulders before. She knew Rita would not wake and that she would have to deal with this alone.

When her tears had stopped she sat up tall and wiped both their faces. Remembering all the good things about the day, she chatted with Rita as though she was awake.

'It was amazing, Rita. We had more excitement than I'd ever dreamed of before this day began. I didn't mean it when I said shop till you drop.' She sighed and smiled, then squeezed Rita's arm, leaned over and kissed her cheek. 'Sleep well.'

Though it was a childish superstition, Vreni whispered their private prayer.

'Now I lay me down to sleep,
I pray the Lord my soul to keep.
And if I die before I wake,
I pray the Lord my soul to take.'

'But you didn't die.' She walked to the door, dimmed the lights and looked back at her sleeping sister. 'But you didn't die.'

—⁂—

The library was warm. Flames ribboned up from the logs in the fireplace, and the familiar smell of books and woollen wall tapestries made Vreni breathe in deeply.

William and Papa were sitting in armchairs, facing each other, each of them holding a glass filled with dark red wine. She walked slowly across to join the conversation. Artūrs entered the room behind her. He was carrying a heavy tray of supper foods.

Papa smiled. 'William has told me about your— evening, Vreni.'

Vreni felt herself unclenching, but she didn't trust herself to speak yet. She sat on a chair next to William. 'He saved us,' she said quietly.

Artūrs took the other two glasses from the small tiled table, handed one to Vreni and sat down opposite her. Vreni looked back at her father. He was staring at her and running his fingers across the pattern cut into his crystal goblet. For now he didn't look like her Papa; instead she saw Parvils, and felt she didn't really know him.

He leaned over and took hold of her hand. 'Please, Vreni,' Papa said. She was suddenly tense. 'Please forgive yourself for today. I am proud of my adventurous daughters.'

She gulped. 'What?'

'I'm not proud of the deception, but I am proud of your spirit. This family is full of strong women who know their own hearts. Following your heart is not always easy, but it's the only way to feel alive. I know a lot about following your heart.'

Papa leaned back in his chair for a brief moment and rubbed his silver wedding amulet between his fingers. He smiled. 'Everyone is safe now, and we have a new person to add to our family, such as it is.' He reached across and patted William solidly on the shoulder.

Vreni's eyes widened. Add to the family? She didn't know what to say.

'Thank you so much for helping us tonight, William,' she stammered. 'I hope everything will be all right with the hospital and—'

Artūrs interrupted with a cough. 'All the loose ends at the hospital have been tidied up,' he said quietly to Parvils.

As the two men nodded at each other, Vreni wondered how they knew about the hospital already. *How had Artūrs known they were on their way home?*

Vreni could see William's face filled with the same questions.

'We've always been a family with ways to—influence others,' Papa said to William. 'Our network, both private and in business, is wide reaching. We have eyes and ears everywhere, especially where my precious daughters are involved. To the world, this night never happened. We can make things happen, and un-happen, as if by magic.' He laughed softly.

Vreni was shocked. *What was Papa thinking? He never spoke so openly about family matters, not even to them. Why was he doing this?*

Vreni watched her father. He looked so at ease, so gracious, yet business like. She felt like an outsider watching a meeting between three businessmen discussing matters in a detached, amiable manner. But this was not just any discussion; it was a secret that so many people had worked so hard to keep for such a very long time. Why was Papa telling this stranger everything?

'So, William, you have noticed by now that our family is unique.' Parvils relaxed back into his chair and stared into his half-filled glass. 'Let me tell you the story of the burden we've carried for more than three centuries. How to begin?'

Parvils paused. 'Of course,' he said with a smile, 'as it should be started. Once upon a time, several centuries ago, there was a fair aristocratic lady named Ieva who loved a kind and wise knight. When they married she was given rule over her family's province. Ieva's evil aunt, Rozālija, was overlooked in the line of succession, and because of this she raged and brewed dark magic, placing a curse on Ieva. When Ieva pricked her skin on the poisoned pin of Rozālija's brooch, she would be trapped in a death-like sleep. No breathing, no heartbeat; not dead but never to wake. Rozālija, also known as Veca Tante, wanted Ieva trapped forever in an *un-place* between life and death, but the other aunties heard of the curse in time to soften the potion—'

'But isn't that the story of Sleeping Beauty?' William said, looking sceptical.

'Yes, Sleeping Beauty.' Parvils nodded. 'That story is our history. Lady Ieva is—was—Vreni's grandmother.'

Artūrs refilled William's glass, and he drank its contents quickly.

'Ieva was my wife's mother. She died seventy years ago, aged sixty-two.' He looked at Vreni. 'Vreni was four years old when her grandmother died. Or were you five?'

'I don't remember, Papa, I was too young.' Vreni watched for William's reaction while she answered her father.

'Seventy years ago, but that would mean —' William stopped and stared at his empty glass. Artūrs filled it once more.

What is Papa doing? Vreni stared at her father, but he simply gestured for her to explain.

'I was born in 1904, and Rita was born two years later,' Vreni said.

'But that's more than a hundred years ago.' William stood and strode across the room. Parvils picked up the bottle and followed. William let him refill his glass while he stared at the fire.

'I told you my daughters were special, and what a shame Gaida, my wife, is asleep. She is so beautiful, like her daughters. She would have enjoyed meeting you. Another time, perhaps.' Papa smiled, but William was still frowning.

'I study science, biochemistry, and this just can't happen. How —' William blustered. 'There isn't any therapy that can extend life like that.'

'Yes, there's some of what you call medicine in the potion—well, herblore and alchemy—but there's also magic,' Parvils said.

'Magic.'

'Of course,' Parvils straightened his shoulders. 'There was more magic in the world then. We don't need it now that we have science. Science is the world's magic now, so the old magic has been diminished, but not for us.'

'So who else is sleeping, Vreni? Why aren't you?' William asked.

'Grandmama Ieva was the first of us.' Vreni felt giddy to think that this discussion could possibly be happening, but she was energised enough to be able to tell her tale and maybe gain William's acceptance.

'In the story, *the fairies, Ieva's aunties,* softened the potion but there was no magical kiss,' she said. 'Ieva did wake, sometimes after sleeping for months or years, and when she was awake she had a normal life, with children and grandchildren. There are five sleepers now: Mama and her two sisters, and Rita and me. We all wake—whenever. 'She shrugged. 'And then we return to long-sleep without warning.'

'Like Rita did,' William whispered. 'What about the husbands? What about you, Parvils?'

'Only the women sleep,' Parvils said. 'The men wait. Ieva's aunts became the Pratigs Māsa, the Wise Sisters, and they gave Vreni's grandfather a precious gift. I received mine when I married Vreni's mother.' He held out his silver amulet. 'With this, the Sisters have slowed time for us.' He blew a kiss toward Vreni. 'Our beauties live a very long time, asleep and awake. The men have a normal lifespan, but by wearing this charm we're granted several lifetimes so we can watch over our beloveds and wait for them to wake.'

Vreni listened to her father talking lovingly about his loyalty to her mother. She thought of dancing with William, and kissing him, and how he had saved her from the attacker. She remembered the feeling of William's kisses on her lips, and wondered how many details Papa knew about their time together. *Why was Papa telling William all these secrets?*

William returned to his chair. Vreni moved to stand beside her father, who was staring at the painting of her mother hanging above the fireplace.

'Papa, why are you saying all this?' she whispered. She glanced towards William. Artūrs was refilling his glass, offering him a tray of cheese, asking him something about horses. 'William seems like a good person but he's still a stranger. Last week you wouldn't even let Rita and me use our real names on the computer and today you're explaining all our secrets to an outsider.'

'When I first met your mother I needed to learn the secrets of this family so I could decide if I was willing to share the burden of the curse,' Parvils said. 'I knew that one day it would be my duty to do the same for another young man.'

'But Papa, we only met *today*,' Vreni hissed.

'And how do you feel about him?'

Vreni thought about spending more time with William, going out dancing again, being normal. Her heart skipped.

'Your eyes are showing me what your heart is starting to feel, and his eyes hold a similar look,' Papa said gently.

Vreni shook her head. 'This doesn't make sense. What if William thinks we're all crazy and decides to tell someone what he's heard?'

'Parvils, the young man is asleep,' Artūrs said, taking the glass from William's limp hand. 'He'll remember nothing. I'll take him home and the car—'

'What? No!' Vreni cried. Her heart thrashed inside her chest. 'Is this why you told him everything, knowing he would remember none of it?'

'I had to be gracious. The young man rescued my daughters.' Papa sounded cool and business like again.

'I was not *rescued*, Papa, I was returned to my prison.' Vreni ground her teeth together tightly, and heat flowed up her face and formed as burning tears. 'I had one normal day, *one day* of living like everyone else does. You said you were proud of having strong daughters, but you punish me so cruelly.'

She clenched her hand around the stem of the glass and flung it away. An explosion of shards flared across the floor. She heard noises behind her and turned to see William being carried from the library.

She crumpled onto a sofa. Sobs rose up in her like crashing waves, threatening to drown her.

—〰—

The fire was dying in the stone hearth when Vreni felt her father's hands on hers. He offered her a soft handkerchief.

'On this day, sweet Vreni, I needed to be the best and the worst father. I am always guided by my loyal promise to protect this family, even if there is pain in my decisions, but no father can watch his daughter's heart break.'

Parvils wrapped her warmly in his arms. 'What we did to William is not your punishment,' he said, 'it is his test. It's the same test I went through. He won't remember when he wakes up, but the memories will still be there, hidden away while his heart decides, and he may remember our secret one day.'

'But he's gone. He's forgotten me.'

'He has not forgotten you. He still has memories of meeting you and dancing,' he said, wiping her tears, 'but he won't remember the rescue or our conversation tonight unless, one day, his heart decides he wants to be part of this life—your life. And then the hidden memories, everything we told him tonight, will be revealed to him.'

'What gives you the right to treat people this way?' Vreni pushed him away angrily.

'It's the way it happened for me when I first knew your mother. I've told your William enough about our family that he might choose to accept his role, and his fate, without any falsehoods, if his heart desires it. The men who join our family need to make their commitment with all of their hearts and minds—no coercion, no secrets. That's the way the Pratigs Māsa insist it must be for the amulets to work.'

'The Sisters?'

'They see something in him,' her father said.

'When did the Sisters see him?'

'This day was full of many watching eyes, and I've come to appreciate the unique quality of the Sisters' perception.'

Vreni thought of the crumpled woman in the cafe who had called Rita 'Sleeping Beauty'. Had she been one of the watchers? Vreni struggled with these stinging truths; the more she knew the more like strangers her family seemed to her.

Vreni looked up at the sound of Sabina's voice. 'This is the way it must be.'

'I will walk in the garden,' Papa said, and left the room.

Sabina took his place beside Vreni.

'So the Wise Sisters are involved in this, of course,' Vreni said. She felt even more naive.

'Yes, Vreni, we needed to made sure that you remained safe.'

'You watched us?'

'Yes, a few of us kept watch while you shopped. Not as well as we would've liked, but your protection charms did their job.'

'So what else am I too young, or stupid, to have worked out about my own life?' Her eyes were hot with new tears.

'You may feel you know nothing, but that's because you haven't needed to know any more until now.' Sabina took her hand warmly. 'Our lives were all changed by the sleeping curse, but life is still life. Even though your life is unique, it's still filled with hope, desires, frustrations and love.'

'Life? What life?'

'This *is* your life, Vreni, but everyone's life has rules and challenges. You're starting a journey towards who you will become. You'll get many chances to make your own decisions, starting tonight.'

'I don't understand,' Vreni said.

'All those centuries ago, the Sisters made a two-fold pledge to your grandmother: firstly to watch over the family, and secondly to one day free you from the sleeping death. We believe we're closer than we've ever been to success in reversing the effects of the potion, but we need to ask you to join in our efforts. We believe you're the one to help us succeed.'

'What good would I be to the sisterhood?' Vreni said bitterly. 'In my one day of independence I put my sister and myself, and our whole family, in peril. I don't believe my efforts would bring you anything but failure, and besides, what does Papa think about all of this?'

Sabina hesitated. 'He sees how important this is and he's proud of you.' She kissed Vreni's forehead tenderly. 'You are much more than you realise right now. You can decide in the morning, but for now you should sleep.'

'Are you staying here tonight?'

'I am.'

Vreni walked with Sabina to the bottom of the stairs. Her tutor headed towards the guest rooms at the back of the house. The evening's feelings of betrayal and doubt were now tangled with curiosity and an excitement about working with the Sisters and what that could mean.

Her feet were heavy on the stairs as she walked to her room. Before today she had felt she didn't belong in the world, and now she barely felt she belonged in her family, but the Sisters were asking her to become another thing.

How could things change so much in one day? What could she possibly do for the Sisters? She didn't even know who they were, except for Sabina. It would be easier to stay in the tower, to stay a sleeping princess. Vreni wondered what the Sisters would ask her to do.

A cool breeze blew off the sea. She watched as the heavy curtains billowed slowly in the moonlight. Finally she slept and dreamed.

My Soul to Take

All is well; young Veronika's resourcefulness
and spirit surpassed our expectations.
Parvils is understandably reticent about
one of his daughters facing such challenges,
but I have asked her to join us. She will
tell me her decision tomorrow.
       ~ Sister Sabina's report to Sister Anna

Almost awake, Vreni lingered in that magical place at the edge of dreaming. She loved real sleep; there were no dreams in the long-sleep of the curse. She drowsed in the warmth of her blankets. Slowly the music in her dream faded and a disturbance somewhere in the house roused her. There was screaming.

She was fully awake now. No, not screaming, wailing, long drawn-out agonised sounds, like an animal in pain.

Vreni was out of her bedroom and running for the source of the sound. The thud of other feet running came from places all over the house, converging on the library.

Pushing through the clot of people in the library doorway, she saw a long-feared scene before her. Her father sat pale and unmoving in his ruddy leather armchair. His eyes were closed. His book, still held in his hand, lay against his chest, open at the last page he was reading.

'Napping, he's just napping.' Vreni whispered.

The stricken wailing coming from her mother was undeniable proof that her father was dead. Gaida had collapsed at her husband's feet, her body convulsing with unspeakable pain. On the other side of the chair, Rita sat curled in a tiny weeping ball, holding Parvils' hand. Vreni's two aunties sat together on the sofa, weeping bitterly.

Vreni wanted go to her father and shake him awake. Then they would all laugh together about acting so foolishly.

'Now I lay me down to sleep,' she whispered as she walked over to her father. She leaned in and kissed him gently on the forehead.

Rita reached up and took her hand, and they finished their prayer together.

'... I pray the lord my soul to take.'

'Oh, Mama, I'm so sorry.' Vreni knelt next to her mother. Holding her, she crooned comforting sounds in Gaida's ear.

'Vreni,' her mother sobbed. 'How horrid this curse is, that it traps me in sleep so long but wakes me to see my Parvils dead. What depths of evil must we endure?'

Vreni held her mother as she shuddered with sadness. They lay together, both leaning, one last time, against the man they loved.

After a while, Mama finally quieted and lay still in Vreni's arms, so still, too still. She realised that her mother had returned to long-sleep. The aunties and Rita were sleeping again too.

The cruelness of the curse struck her again; even the softened potion brimmed with evil, taking the sleepers away from so much of life's pleasure but waking them to experience pain. Vreni knew that when Mama woke next, the pain of her husband's death would be fresh once again, like an open wound. Gaida would not have the solace of a final goodbye at her husband's funeral.

Vreni stared down at her mother's sleeping eyes, swollen from weeping, the tears of grief still wet on her quiescent cheeks.

'I will not live this way,' Vreni hissed.

She untangled herself from her mother and walked to the corner of the library. She watched Artūrs scoop her sleeping mother into his arms to take her back to her accursed bed.

Who will watch over us now? Vreni wiped away her burning tears.

'I will not live this way,' she whispered again as she followed Artūrs out of the library.

She rushed out the front door into the cool morning mist. 'I will not live this way,' she shouted.

Sobs rose up in her throat, and she gulped them down. Her chest heaved as if her heart might disintegrate with grief. She ran stumbling through the garden until she reached the small pinegrove her father had planted. She wrapped her arms around the thickest trunk.

The bark spiked her face as she pressed hard into its roughness, weeping.

'I will not live this way!'

—⁓—

Finally, Vreni returned to the house and went up to the tower. She stood staring out at the sea. She watched the birds diving for fish and remembered other times on the beach. Frosty walks on the gritty beaches near Vārve, bracing against a sudden chill wind and sheltering behind her father. She thought of their last day on the beach together with the new ponies. Days like that would never happen again.

Her breath came in sobs. *Did my choices yesterday do this to Papa?* She had run through the garden trying to run from the pain, from the way her life would be now, but she knew she could not run from her life, only change it. Her tears dried into salty streaks on her face as she watched the gentle rise and fall of the sea beyond the cliffs.

I need to do this thing Sabina has asked me to do, whatever it is, if it will free us. Without Papa, it's up to me to keep us safe.

'Vreni, I cannot know your pain, but I can share your loss,' Sabina said, appearing at the top of the tower stairs. She took Vreni in her arms and they sat down together on the top step. Rocking her gently, Sabina began to hum.

Vreni let the quiet music soak into her and fill some of the emptiness. 'I can't live this life.'

'We don't want you to live this way, either. We believe we can lift the curse, but we need you to help, so on this day, when I know you're already carrying such a heavy load, I must add to it by asking you to decide.'

Sabina wiped away tears from both their faces.

'How can I help you?' Vreni asked. 'I've never even noticed who, or what, you really are.'

'For as long as your family has laboured under the curse, the Wise Sisters have promised to protect you and to someday free you of the curse. Our Watch-Haven Trust has traded and invested to ensure we have the funds to keep our promises. Through the trust we have woven a far-reaching web, and we have seen that the Alchemists Guild, which Veca Tante brought into being to serve her wicked purposes has also endured, although it is now called AlGuild. We continue to watch them and soften the corporate harm they cause when we can.'

'So what do you need from me?'

'We're very close now, Vreni. We're sure we can reverse the potion completely and free you all from the sleeping death. What I ask is for you to help us achieve this wonderful thing for your family and for you.'

'But I don't have anything to offer.'

'There's more to you than you can know yet, young Vreni. It's time for you to come and join the Sisters at Mežs Mājas, our forest home. Let us teach you and show you who you really are.'

Vreni looked out at the darkening sky and realised that this saddest of days was ending. 'I will join you,' she said, leaning her exhausted body into Sabina.

They descended the tower stairs without speaking and walked to Vreni's bedroom. Sabina tucked the blankets tightly around Vreni and sat next to her with the light of the waning moon shining weakly through the curtains. Sabina hummed quietly until Vreni slept.

Choice

*When the cage door lies open, what
choices does the bird make by
spreading her wings to take flight?*

~ *Book of Questions*

Vreni stood in the early-morning stillness of the house that had been her haven and protection ever since arriving in this new country with its harsh sun and topsy-turvy seasons. She let her thoughts drift off to the snowy winters left behind, and could almost feel her cheeks burning from the icy wind dashing across her face as she rode in the open wagon.

How long ago was that? At least half a century, if she went by the way everyone else measured time. Perhaps soon she would measure time in this way as well.

She walked slowly through the house. It felt like a mausoleum, with all the people she loved trapped in the cocoon of long-sleep. She climbed the stairs to the bedrooms until even the small noises from downstairs melted away, leaving nothing but a stifling silence that seemed to eat at her spirit.

She stood looking down from the top of the stairs towards the library door.

Her father would lay forever in the pine grove he had planted to remind him of his old home. He had spent years in this house, and in their chalet back in Vārve, watching over his wife, longing for her to wake and be with him.

Did he jump at every unexpected noise, hoping it was one of them waking? Vreni tried to imagine the stillness her father had lived with as he marked time. He had been their protector, but now it was time for her to take his place. She vowed to do whatever it took to free them from the endless heartbreak of the curse.

Fragments of memories from Sabina's lessons had started to reveal themselves. Songs, curious rhymes, the ancient traditions of nature craft and folk lore bubbled into her awareness, and she felt there was more hiding just out of reach. Apprehension made her hands damp, but she felt eager to discover how the old magic of the Wise Sisters would change her life.

Sabina had said the Sisters would teach Vreni the skills and secrets she needed to play her part in creating the cure. All she could do now was put her faith in the Sisters; she had no other choice.

Things had to change. Papa was gone. Artūrs would safeguard the sleepers for now, but she would have to become their protector soon.

She imagined William waiting, guarding her. She couldn't ask anyone who loved her to wait and wither while she slept.

Maybe one day he would love her enough to wear the amulet, but she knew she would not ask that, not after watching her father live as love's prisoner, and seeing the pain in her mother's eyes as she watched Papa growing older and older each time she woke.

What an obligation Mama must feel. Vreni knew she would hate being weighed down with such a debt.

Her footsteps fell silently on the thick carpeting as she walked along the landing looking in at her family. She said her goodbyes to her sleeping aunties. It was much simpler that they all slept, leaving her awake and freer than she had ever been before. She took it as a positive sign that her *quest* with the Wise Sisters would be successful. Even if it didn't succeed, to try anyway and fail would be more acceptable to Vreni than doing nothing.

She entered the silent room where Gaida was sleeping and lay down next to her mother as she sometimes did when she missed her very badly.

'Stay asleep, Mama. If you wake now you'll stop me doing what I have to do. Stay asleep a little longer, and when you wake the curse will be over.' She kissed her mother's smooth forehead and walked from the room.

Rita's room was full of colour and comfort, with walls of posters, shoes strewn on the floor and too many cushions. Rita lay in her bed looking like she might wake at any minute.

'Hey, Rita, do you want to come with me? I'm getting out of the house again, and this time I get to stay away for a while.' She looked at her sister, wishing that shaking her would wake her up. She pressed her hands into tight fists, feeling her fingers tingle when she relaxed them. 'If the Wise Sisters are successful, this might be your last long-sleep.' She sat down and pushed up close to her sister. 'I wish you would wake and come with me. I know I'd be less scared if you were there …'

Vreni let out a slow breath, and leaned over and kissed her sister's cheek. Tasting a trace of saltiness from Rita's tears for their father, she stiffened, stood quickly and rushed to the door. She turned and forced a smile.

'I'm sure I won't be going shopping, so I'm sorry, but I won't be able to bring you any shoes. I'll see you soon, Rita.'

She walked back down the silent stairs. She was leaving the sanctuary of her home for the unknown that lay ahead. *Could they all die, sleeping here like this?* Vreni had never thought of her family being unsafe before.

'Now I lay me down to sleep,' she whispered, ' I pray the lord my soul to keep, and if I die before I wake, I pray the lord my soul to take.'

Vreni knew her family was safe for now, with Artūrs and the few others who ran the house protecting them, but she was also their guardian now.

Possibility was power, Sabina had told her. A person's intentions hold power and when those intentions were combined with faith and action, miracles could be achieved. That would mean the intention placed on a spell, and then woven into the words spoken over a potion or an amulet, could turn the desire of the spellmaker into reality.

Am I a spellmaker? I need faith, like the bird that sings before the sun rises; I need to believe because belief is the true power.

She shuddered as another clutch of forgotten fragments from Sabina's lessons popped into her head. What else would she need to become? All she could do was ask Sabina.

MežsMājas

Even in the dense summer forest the birds
that should be together can always find each
other. Together they are always stronger.

~ Book of Wisdom

Now that it was time, Vreni could not close the front door behind her.

'Artūrs and the others are here,' Sabina said soothingly, 'and the Wise Sisters will watch as they have always watched.' She put her hand on Vreni's and, as the car sent from the sisterhood pulled up in the driveway, closed the door on the only life Vreni had known.

They stood for a moment outside the closed door in the morning sun. Vreni thought that Sabina looked different now than she had done during lessons. She was softer somehow, as though she had taken off a rigid mask of herself.

Sabina smiled and warmly clasped both of Vreni's hands in her own. 'Welcome, Sister Veronika, I am Sister Sabina,' she said as though they were meeting for the first time. 'May our strength be your strength.' She kissed Vreni on one cheek and then the other.

Vreni felt the honour in this formal greeting, like she was becoming part of something astonishing. The sense of otherness, the feeling of being isolated she had known for so long, was disappearing. She belonged with the Sisters, not as a child but as the woman she was becoming.

—⁂—

Vreni was quiet in the car as it sped through the stark landscape. The unforgiving glare of the sun seemed to bleach the colour out of the scrawny trees and bushes that struggled to push up out of the dry ground. The brightness even threatened to fade the blue from the sky itself.

She opened her window and felt the blast of dry air in her face. It smelled of overheated dust and some unknown woody spice. Her ears rang with the ceaseless squeal of some mysterious insect. She closed the window and returned to the cool quiet of her thoughts.

The car finally turned from the smooth black strip of highway and began snaking its way up through a cluster of parched hills. As they rounded a dusty bend, Vreni could see that the narrow road passed between two large boulders. Beyond the boulders she saw a glimpse of green, not organised and potted colour like at home or in the city, but greens of every hue, stretching on and on. She sat forward as the car passed through the gap between the boulders and dropped down into an immense, lush valley. Her breath caught in her throat; these were like the colours of summer in Vārve.

The thin road swept through pine and birch and moss that cascaded down the slopes on all sides. Shaded patches full of summer mushrooms were surrounded by thick tangles of emerald ferns. Here and there she saw woody, dark green canes laden with glistening red berries. There was bird song and bumblebees, and the smell of the dampness in the earth after the snow has melted.

But this should all be decades ago and half a world away from where we are now. Vreni gazed around, devouring the sights. She hadn't realised until now how much she had hungered for this. The car followed the curving road and eventually emerged from the deep teals and jades into a rolling grassy field dotted with small yellow flowers. At the centre of the field sat a ring of buildings.

'Welcome to Mežs Mājas.'

'Forest home,' Vreni whispered.

Sabina squeezed her hand. 'We thought you would enjoy how this place looks.'

'You're right, but how —'

'At Mežs Mājas, and at some other places where we prevail, it's up to the Sisters what the world we weave looks like. So we create what we desire. We seek our comfort by weaving a place like this that is truly ours. For so many centuries the Wise Sisters lived as part of the old forests; we knew the secrets of the plants, spoke the language of each creature and shared the songs of the birds. It's all part of us and we could not be removed from it all so easily. The forests and the creatures they nurture are within our hearts, and therefore they are ours to weave as we desire.'

'Magic,' Vreni said.

Sabina shrugged and nodded, then looked into the rear-vision mirror and caught the eye of the woman driving, as if looking for reassurance.

'You will learn to be a weaver of worlds too, Sister Veronika,' the woman said, 'a bringer of victory.'

Not Vreni, but Veronika. A bringer of victory? She felt hot. Her heart leapt in her chest. 'I will be her,' she whispered. *I want to be this person, this bringer of victory. I've lain sleeping too long.*

The car slowed and stopped in front of a long stone cottage, the pitched roof a thick blanket of thatch that pointed up into the lavender-blue sky. Woven baskets full of vibrantly coloured geraniums hung from the eaves.

At the edge of the circle of cottages stood a tall windmill, its sails rotating lazily in the gentle breeze. Vreni tried to see inside the cottages but the rows of lead-paned windows only mirrored the trees. She stepped from the car, her footfalls crunching on the gravel driveway. She caught herself looking for a stork's nest in the chimney pots. Storks were bringers of harmony and good fortune for the households where they choose to nest.

'Yes, we even have storks,' said the driver, the woman who had called her Veronika. 'Welcome to Mežs Mājas, I am Sister Anna. We want this place to feel like home for you.

Sabina and I will make sure you feel happy here. We'll also guide you as you prepare for your task.'

Vreni cringed. *Guide and prepare her for what?* She met Anna's fiery blue eyes and, reached out with both hands, greeted Anna and kissed her. 'Thank you, this is already more than I'd dreamed of.'

'If you can dream it then it can be so,' Anna said. 'Welcome home.'

Flanked by her new companions, Vreni walked to the door of the cottage.

The interior was filled with soft light that rippled through the uneven glass in the windows. The walls were white and roughly plastered. Colourful tapestries hung on the walls, showing scenes brimming with the birds and animals of the forest. The colours were bold and lively, and the animal figures seemed almost to be moving and going about the job of gathering food and feeding their babies.

A wooden table ran the length of the room underneath the windows on the far side, beyond which was a sun-drenched courtyard garden. The long table was covered with a beautiful white cloth that had an intricate pattern woven into it. Along the centre of the table sat numerous platters and dishes, some made of wood, some of silver, and laden with meats, chicken and cheese. There were bowls of steaming soup and baskets of bread, dumplings and sweet pastry.

Vreni had eaten very little since her father had died. Grief had filled her stomach with rocks. But she knew that refusing to eat, or eating like a mouse, would be ungracious of her, and the aromas rising from the food were unexpectedly tantalizing.

A noisy gaggle of young girls suddenly burst through the door. They were laughing and jostling each other.

'Young sisters, please settle yourselves, you chirp like hungry chicks,' Anna called over the noise. 'Come and meet our newest fledgling, Vreni—I mean Veronika—is Sister Sabina's niece. We all know how first days feel, so please help her feel welcome.'

'Hello,' Vreni said nervously. 'This is all so beautiful, I'm so pleased to be here.'

She braced herself, wondering if the girls knew who she was, and how they would react. But they rapidly surrounded her, offering outstretched hands to shake and warm pecks on her cheek. She was relieved and pleased to just be one of the new birds.

Their voices grew louder again as they swept Vreni towards the table. They sat down, surrounding her, and started eating. Vreni felt lighter inside because of the warmth of their welcome, and the rocks she had felt in her stomach were replaced with her old appetite. The food was divine and Vreni was relieved to realise that all of the young sisters were far too busy interrupting each other to ask her any questions. It was like being at a table full of Ritas, all talking excitedly at the same time.

—⁂—

After lunch the young sisters invited Vreni to join them as they went for an afternoon of practising what they had learned in the morning's lessons. The girls dawdled through the circular garden to another low building they called the lab.

Inside, the lab was cool and sparsely furnished, with tall stools circling a large, heavy marble-topped bench. In the centre of the bench were piles of dried herbs tied in bundles, jars of seeds and spices, and bowls of dried flower petals. A metal box contained small glass bottles, a few of which were filled with coloured liquids. Each girl had a heavy stone mortar and pestle in front of her.

Vreni took a seat at the bench.

'Dill seed in your bath water makes you *irresistible*,' a girl named Sofia said, and giggled. Her blue eyes shone as she lifted a few dill seeds and sprinkled them onto the tabletop, and then passed the jar of seeds around the table.

Vreni inhaled the fresh smell.

'The scent of cloves on your skin, and your love will do whatever you ask him to,' another girl, Emma, said with a laugh.

They passed the afternoon mixing ointments and fragrant herbal potions, mostly useful only for attracting boys. Vreni felt familiar and confident with the work. Again, there were flashes of memory from Sabina's jumbled lessons. The fragrances she worked with that afternoon smelt similar to some that belonged to her mother or her aunties. She and Rita had dabbed them on themselves when they were younger and played dress-ups, and she had worn one of them on her trip into the city.

Cloves? William had taken risks to help her that night. Maybe the fragrance had come from the Sisters. Maybe William had only been attentive and helpful because of some potion. Vreni shook her head, feeling overly suspicious.

'So you're Sabina's niece,' Sofia said.

'Yes,' Vreni said, relieved that she didn't need to create a story. 'And she's my—tutor,' she added.

'You've had extra spellwork then, lucky you. Has she shown you the chants for growing things yet? I can't wait to get my own whisper birds.'

'No,' Vreni said, wondering what Sofia was talking about. 'We've been concentrating on herbs.'

'That's why you're so good at these,' Emma said.

Vreni looked down and realised she had been mixing while she was talking, and the lotion in her mortar was glowing with energy and resonating with a quiet hum. The girls fell silent and joined with the tone of the hum.

'They're always more powerful if we all give voice to the intention,' Sofia said. 'Seal it in the jar while it's full of energy.'

Vreni wasn't sure what she had intended, but she spooned the humming mixture into a blue glass jar and sealed it. *I have magic inside me, and all around me.*

Vreni worked and watched, getting to know the other girls, who were mostly the daughters of the Wise Sisters. The end of the afternoon's experimentation was signalled by the sound of song rising throughout the gardens.

The young sisters quickly packed away their herbs, petals and bottles, and left the lab. They joined in the singing and followed behind the older women. Vreni followed and copied. She knew the songs as soon as she heard them and wondered how this could be, but the questions were washed from her mind by the rising music.

As the sun set, the Sisters gathered together in the circular courtyard garden and sang for the blessing of the day and to welcome Vreni. She felt the rhythms and the power of the songs became part of her.

The days that followed were a whirl of old traditions, charms and magic. Vreni realised that Sabina had somehow been weaving lore and magical skills into her daily lessons for a long time, because the concentrated training at Mežs Mājas seemed to trigger a knowing deep within her. She felt as though she was discovering new but ancient things, gifts from the past that had lain dormant inside her until being here had stirred them into life, but she still felt sure there was more that remained unknown to her.

Glimmer

A glimmer will only hold back hidden memories
if the glimmered mind allows it; once a person
wishes the memories to surface, the glimmer
will not hold for long against their free will,
but a guided awakening is always kinder.

~ Book of Wisdoms

'**Tell** me what you've hidden in me,' Vreni said to Sabina as they walked among the curving rows of fruit trees.

Sabina looked across at Anna, who was walking through a small orchard gathering ripe fruit. Vreni also watched Anna as she murmured words of thanks to each tree for its gifts before placing the fruit in the basket. Anna looked up from her whisperings and started towards them. Sabina nodded, and then guided Vreni through the garden.

'Understand, Vreni, that we're all linked by the wisdom of the old magic. I trained you and Rita during your recent awakenings in the hope that one of you would show the strength and skill for our undertaking. This training would have been a large burden to place on a child who already carries so much, so we decided to conceal your lessons within a *glimmer*, so the magic could remain hidden in the back of your awareness until we knew you were ready to embrace your potential.'

'Glimmer? Training?' Vreni's mind tumbled with questions.

'Be patient, and you'll be able to answer all your own questions once the *glimmer* is lifted.'

They reached the edge of a still pond, which was ringed with heavy square stones. Anna joined them and lowered her basket to the grass. Sabina beckoned Vreni to sit on a stone bench that faced the unmoving water. Vreni placed her palms on the cool stone, watching the colours of the garden reflected on the water.

'We can see the smooth water, but some things are hidden just below the surface.' Anna's voice was smooth.

'If the surface is all you seek, then that is all you will see,' Sabina added.

'Within your glimmer lies wisdom and power ...'

'... insight and control ...'

'... burden and challenge ...'

Vreni felt encircled by the Sisters' words, as though she was contained in a bubble. Everything was still.

'Do you choose to see below the surface of your glimmer?' Sabina said. 'To see who you can be?'

'I do,' Vreni whispered.

A faint hum began to rise from Sabina and Anna, their voices overlapping in a weave of tone upon rhythm. The rhythm seeped into Vreni's chest and she felt her heart following its beat. Anna began to lay her words on top of

Sabina's echoing chant. Vreni felt the bubble surrounding her filling with the power of the words. She breathed them in.

'Look beneath to see within,
to where true vision hides.
See beneath and look within,
to where your truth abides.'

When Anna finished speaking, she picked up a smooth pebble and handed it to Vreni. Vreni rubbed the pebble slowly between her thumb and fingers, and threw it. It dropped into the glassy surface of the pond.

There was a sudden release of pressure as the bubble that had surrounded her burst. Her awareness was flooded with the hot energy of knowing. Secrets sprang from their hiding places in the back of her mind, and she could now hear echoes of songs and chants and words of power.

Images of what she had written in her forgotten journal flashed into her mind. She saw pages filled with spells, and formulas for gain and influence. She could smell and taste—*dill seed, clove, sorrel*—the herbs and unctions that she had mixed and laced with the intent of her heart's desire. There was a fresh knowing, of the secret hiding places in the linings of her clothes, where she had hidden her personal talismans—*garnet for protection, cat's eye to remain unseen*—and the words she had used to enchant them echoed in her ears.

She drew a sharp, painful breath. It felt for a moment like she was awakening from long-sleep.

The smooth coolness of the stone bench was the first thing Vreni noticed as the flood of revealed knowledge ebbed back into the places it had been stored, but now it was no longer hidden from her. She felt remade but also familiar and complete. She sighed, rising from the stone seat.

'I will become Veronika, bringer of victory. I am no longer just Vreni, sleeping princess.' She stood tall.

'She remembers,' Sabina said.

'You've done well, Sisters.' Anna smiled at them, and from within her basket of fruit she took a thick tattered book with a bright blue leather cover. 'This is yours, Sister Veronika.'

When she handed Vreni the blue book, Vreni remembered that it held all the knowledge from her hidden lessons.

Now I Lay Me Down to Sleep

*'It is recorded in the Book of Wisdom
that a youngling will travel into the
dream realm and return safely.'
'But how can we be sure that the traveller is her?'
'We cannot be sure, but we can hope.'*

~ Conversation between Sister
Sabina and Sister Anna

On the night of the second full moon since she had arrived at Mežs Mājas, Sabina and Anna led Vreni out to the central courtyard that was lit by the milky light of the newly risen moon. They walked through the lush garden to a darkened corner where a doorway glowed. Inside it looked like a small rock grotto. Sabina beaconed Vreni to enter.

As Vreni's eyes became accustomed to the soft light, she saw that she was at the top of a helical staircase that led below ground. She thought of the spirals hidden within seashells, and stood for a moment, letting her eyes blur and play tricks with the shadows and dimensions of the glowing helix.

Sabina placed a hand on her shoulder.

'What's down there?' Vreni asked.

'A place where we have access to the Realm of Dreams that connects us all across place and time.'

'Dreams?'

'Come, we'll show you,' Anna said.

Vreni felt the warmth of the rough stone steps against her feet as they descended in silence. At the base of the stairs was a doorway filled with warm light. Vreni felt the slight resistance of an unseen wall of energy as she stepped over the threshold. A circle of Sisters stood in the centre of the room. Their singing filled the air. The rhythmic threads wove in and out of each other, creating a fabric of sound that rippled around her.

'Spirals within circles, within circles making spirals,
Dreams circle our hearts and spiral from our minds.
We spiral within so we may circle without.
Journeys within journeys, endings and beginnings.'

Vreni walked around the chamber, running her hand along the smooth, curving stone wall. It was alive with colour: paintings of trees, flowers, herb plants and animals were all part of a beautiful circular garden. Within this colourful garden, painted women were dancing, their faces full of joy and their hands raised up to the sky. Vreni expected to see them move and join in with the other voices in the room.

She followed the gaze of the painted eyes that were looking towards the ceiling, and saw a spiral of sparkling light that started near the door and wound around and around, growing finer as it coiled towards a glowing crystal at its centre. Vreni moved to the rhythm of the music and muttered the songs as she followed the curving wall back to the door.

'What is this place?' she asked.

'It's a dream room,' Sabina said. 'We're here to continue your preparation and training, and to give you your first challenge.'

The circle of Sisters parted, and Vreni noticed a raised platform in the centre of the room. She shuddered and looked quickly to Sabina. 'Dream room?'

'Yes, we're going to make you sleep,' Sabina said. Seeing Vreni turn pale, she added, 'Not long-sleep, just a nap.' She took Vreni's hand.

'By entering the Dream Realm,' Anna said, 'you can travel back to the time of the cursing, feel the power of it, and, we hope, find the original potion. We've tried sending others to find it, but they can't sense it.'

'You are your dreams, and your dreams are you,' Sabina said. 'We believe you will feel the potion because you have the traces of it in your blood. You need to seek out the original potion and hold it in your hand, to feel and remember the dread.'

'But why?' Vreni asked.

'Because that memory will bring us a little closer to the cure,' Sabina said.

Vreni's heart fluttered as she looked at the sleeping platform. 'What will happen? What will I do?'

'We believe the alchemists hid the remainder of Veca Tante's potion once they had painted it on every sharp object they hoped Ieva might touch.' Anna patted Vreni's hand and smiled. 'In the dream realm you'll visit your grandmother's palace. The alchemists had secret chambers that faced the setting sun, and the potion will be hidden somewhere in there. You will appear to be a scullery maid, one of many, expected only to scrub and fetch, so you'll be able to move about unnoticed,' Anna said reassuringly.

'Just a few weeks ago I couldn't even rescue my own sister without help.' Vreni's throat was tight. 'There'll be no one with me this time, so how will I do it on my own?'

'You'll have tools and spells to aid you,' Sabina said soothingly. 'The sisters always left a cache of charms and spells in case one of their own was caught in need. Our chambers were—are—on the side of the castle that faces the morning sun. In those chambers, look for a box within a box within a box.' Sabin apointed toward the ceiling. 'It will be marked with a spiral that only Sisters can see. Inside you'll find a veil of silk, a circle of mirrored silver, a pouch filled with what look like tiny seeds—'

'Cloth, a mirror, seeds? How will those things help?' Vreni snapped. Her stomach churned.

'The seeds are the eggs of whisper birds,' Sabina said. 'Sprinkle some into your hand, whisper your heart's desire and they'll hatch and grow to do your bidding before they fly to freedom. When you wear the mirror charm around your neck you'll be invisible to all but those skilled in old magic.

The silk veil is infused with a taming potion. It will calm beasts and people when it's laid upon them. You are of the Pratigs Māsa, Vreni; the time for doubt is gone. The time of magic is here.'

Thoughts of running back up the stairs tempted Vreni. She stood frozen for a long moment, and then walked towards the raised platform. Lying on the warm stone, she stared up at the glistening spiral. The rhythmic chanting of the Sisters rose up and filled her awareness. She felt the heaviness of sleep approaching.

Now I lay me down to sleep ...

Realm of Dreams

~ Pratigs Māsa, *Book of Wisdoms*

This awakening was different: there was none of the burning like after long-sleep, and no warm dreaminess either; she was suddenly awake and alert. Vreni lay with her eyes half closed, listening to the clatter of cooking and many busy voices. Her nose twitched at the stale-smelling pile of straw and cloth remnants that made up her makeshift bed on the floor next to a warm stone hearth.

'Wake up,' said a voice next to her. 'Hurry, *steigā*, the day is half over already.' A hand shoved at her and she opened her eyes fully.

'Come on, my lazy friend,' said the smiling girl.

'Good morning,' Vreni said, expecting the girl to question who she was, but she just gestured towards the crowded worktables.

I am me, but I am not me. Vreni stood and smoothed her rough woollen dress, brushing the straw from its folds. Sabina had said that while she travelled in the dream realm she would just be a suggestion at the edge of peoples' minds. And how could she be anything else when she wouldn't even be born for centuries to come? But this place was real enough. If it weren't, the Sisters wouldn't have told her about the box of magic left ready in case she needed it.

Vreni followed the smiling girl and copied her actions. She took a boiled egg and ate it hurriedly, washing it down with a cup of clabbered milk, wincing as she swallowed. It was Papa's favourite drink, but she had never liked the sour taste.

'These are for the high table,' the smiling girl said.

Vreni watched closely and again copied. The girl took a tray of breads. Vreni took the second tray full of smoked fish and cheese, and followed her through the stone doorway towards a large hall.

As they approached the table, Vreni caught sight of her grandmother. Grandmama Ieva was so beautiful, so full of grace and kindness. The tray Vreni was carrying tilted and almost fell. She struggled to calm herself.

Grandmama Ieva sat next to her husband Carls, and there were others seated around the table. She could not take her eyes from her grandmother. Their gaze met for a moment as Vreni placed the tray on the table.

'Thank you, sweet one,' Ieva said as she smiled and picked up the tray to serve her guests.

Grandmama looks so young and happy. Vreni kept busy with small jobs so she could stay and watch for a while, and then walked back to the kitchen smiling.

When the flurry of breakfast was over, Vreni picked up rags and a wooden bucket and made her way outside. She stood at the well as if gathering water, all the while using the direction of the sun to orient herself to the location of the apartments in the east and west of the palace. She set out first toward the morning sun in search of the box within a box within a box that could contain her salvation if today's searching became complicated or dangerous.

Watching to ensure she remained unnoticed, she made her way steadily eastwards through the cool, damp passageways that twisted through the palace. Away from the cooking fires, the air was chilled, and the slender arrow-slits in the thick stone walls allowed only choked rays of light to penetrate the gloom. She carried her rags and bucket with an air of purpose in case she was being observed.

Door after locked door yielded nothing. Finally she saw a faint glow in an alcove up ahead. On a door was a small spiral; it was there for a moment and then faded. She turned the door's handle and it opened for her.

Inside, the room was flooded with morning light. She stood like a startled animal, waiting for her eyes to adjust to the brightness. Although she believed she would have been welcome, she was still relieved that the room was empty. This day and this challenge was hers alone. She was the girl who did not belong here, and she did not want to cause complications or danger for the Wise Sisters who had been—or would be—so loyal and protective of her family.

Vreni calmed her mind and opened her perception to the search.

'A box within a box, within a box,' she muttered. But there were several boxes in the room. This room could be the first box. Out of the corner of her eye she saw a spark of light as a second spiral flared and glowed, then faded swiftly. 'Blessings!'

She ran towards the chest by the window and opened it. Inside were two rough woollen dresses, a bundle of linen rags and a leather journal. She lifted these items gently and discovered a small birch-wood box. She ran her hand over the smoothly polished lid, which glowed momentarily with a spiral.

Lifting out the smaller box, she closed the larger one and sat on its lid with the small birch-wood box on her lap. Her heart sank when she opened it; the box contained nothing but herbs. Why was this box marked for her to find if its contents were useless to her?

Vreni searched into her newly remembered training and stopped herself before fear and doubt could cloud her thinking. 'Show the truth I seek.' She spoke the words quietly.

Around the edges of the box she saw a faint glow. She loosened the herb tray and lifted it out. Underneath was a compartment holding a cloth of silk, an amulet and a small pouch, just as she had been told.

But how could they be here? The box wasn't deep enough to have a hidden compartment. Vreni shook her head in wonder. 'I have much to learn.'

She was about to leave when she recalled another thing. She must give a sign of thanks to the *Pratigs Māsa for providing her with these charms and potions.* She knelt next to the chest she had been sitting on and, using the tip of her finger, drew two circles on a polished lid, a smaller one inside a larger one, with the two circles touching at a single point.

'It was given freely, received with gratitude,' she said, 'and it will return to you three times over.'

With the small box placed in her bucket and covered with cleaning rags, Vreni left the peaceful room belonging to the Sisters she would never meet and, with hesitant steps, started westward in search of the alchemists' chambers.

After the quiet of home, and even the purposeful bustle of her time at Mežs Mājas, Vreni was amazed by the crowds that filled the palace. So many people were engaged in household tasks and running messages. She realised that she was looking at this world through her modern eyes. Without technology and machines, it took a lot of people to do all the work.

While everyone was busy dealing with visitors coming and going, Vreni entered a room. She gasped and hid herself in a shadowy corner. Her grandmother was there, overseeing preparations for her guests. *She looked so happy.* Today Vreni had seen that being welcoming and hospitable was a pleasure for her family, and she knew from family stories that for Ieva, being taken from all this was the greatest tragedy of the curse. Was *there a chance she could stop it all happening?*

Her mind raced with possibilities. She searched for a secluded place to think. In a corner in the palace's central courtyard was a kitchen garden; she sat among the scraggy, overgrown herbs out of sight and pondered.

Grandmama's not sleeping yet. I could find the potion and destroy it before we're cursed. My family would be free. 'Why didn't the Sisters speak to me about this possibility?' she whispered.

Vreni opened the borrowed box. She took out the mirrored silver amulet, tying the smooth silk ribbon it hung on around her neck. She unfolded the silk cloth and draped it around her hips so it appeared to be an apron. Then she loosened the string on the pouch. It was filled with small, pale seeds. She let one seed fall into the palm of her hand.

Placing her lips close to the grain in her hand, she whispered, 'Show me. Teach me.'

The surface of the seed smoothed and was now an egg. The minuscule egg cracked open. A tiny robin hatched out, fluffed up its minute feathers and doubled and redoubled in size until it was fully grown. It turned to look at Vreni for a moment and, nodding its tiny head, flew from her hand and landed on a flowering sorrel bush.

'Amazing,' Vreni said, as she tucked the pouch of seeds into the pocket hidden in the fold of her dress. 'Thank you for the lesson, young robin.' She gestured the sign of thanks on the lid of the box and left it to be found in the garden.

The palace was a maze of darkened passageways that opened out unexpectedly into light-filled halls and galleries that were filled with the sound of banter talk of business and trade, domestic scuttling, and laughter and music.

Vreni made her way westward. With the freedom of invisibility that the amulet offered her, she allowed her curiosity to rule her for a short while. She watched the girls in the kitchen, who looked to be about the same age as her. They were talking about new dresses, gossiping about a look from a boy, or a flower left as a token of love. Gossiping, just as she and Rita did.

Many hours seemed to pass as Vreni explored the palace, observing her family's history while she hid behind the mirror amulet's magic.

In the western most wing of the palace, she rounded a sweeping curve in the passageway and heard voices. Daring to look, she saw a stick-thin old man talking to a young guard. She saw from the ornate pin on the collar of the old man's robes that he was an alchemist.

'No one enters or leaves without my word. Except Rozālija, of course,' the alchemist said.

'Of course, sire, the old aunt pleases herself,' the young guard replied.

'Indeed she does.' The alchemist laughed as he walked away down the passageway, his laughter diminishing.

Vreni stepped forward around the bend, waiting to see if the amulet made her invisible to the guard. She came so close to the man that she could smell the smoked fish he'd eaten for breakfast on his breath. She wrinkled her nose. He couldn't see her, but he was blocking the door and stopping her entering the alchemists' chamber.

Recollecting a spell for casting voice, she prepared to conjure the alchemist's words to play with the guard's perceptions. Taking a slow, quiet breath, she recalled the tone of the alchemist's voice and then spoke, sending the conjured voice far off into the dim passageway.

'I have stumbled, damn these uneven stones,' the conjured voice echoed.

The young guard turned his head toward the voice and walked into the gloom.

Vreni took the moment and pushed open the heavy door just wide enough, slipping into the chamber.

The room was lit by a single stripe of pale light coming from a tall, arched window. Motes of dust drifted across the band of sunshine. The walls of the chamber were lined with shelves laden with books, boxes and bottles. Wooden benches were cluttered with strange pieces of equipment that looked like they belonged in some frightening black-and-white movie. The air smelled of an odd blend of sweet oils made by crushing herbs and flowers, along with something much less appealing, something that reminded Vreni of the smell of sweaty horses.

She heard a muffled rasping sound and walked forward slowly, straining to hear it again. She scanned the room cautiously, and her throat tightened.

Lying asleep on a small bed under the window were three children, girls who looked barely seven years old. *These girls can't be here. What will they do to them?*

She rushed over and sat on the bed, shaking the girls' shoulders. She put her mouth close to their ears. 'Wake up,' she whispered harshly, trying to rouse them without alerting the guard.

Then she knew they could not have made the noise she had heard. These girls would not wake, not ever. The potion had been used on them: not the softened one but the true sleeping-death potion.

'They sleep alone. No one knows to watch over them,' she whispered. A warm tear ran down her cheek. A sudden wave of outrage washed over her. How many more girls like this were there? She wiped the tear away roughly, determined to find the potion.

Moving back across the room, she began scouring the shelves filled with bottles, searching for markings that would identify the potion, reaching out with her intuition to feel with her heart and her mind.

At last Vreni felt drawn towards a small tear-shaped bottle made of blue glass. On the outside of the bottle was a stained leather label, on which had been drawn a picture of a sleeping face; the rest of the figure in the drawing was shown bound tightly with dark rope.

'Binding the victim in the prison of the sleeping death,' Vreni muttered, picking up the almost-empty bottle.

A burning cold crept up her arm. Her heart trembled with uncertain, fast-slow rhythms. Dark sounds wailed in her ears. She wanted to drop the bottle and be free from the cold of it, but her hand was frozen and would not release its grip. The bottle was nearly empty, and the potion had already been put where it would do its evil deed.

Catch Me If You Can

'**Ah,** someone else who will sleep and never die,' a voice boomed behind Vreni.

Her face flooded with heat. The alchemist had returned. He was standing by the closed door. Next to him stood a willowy woman with burning amber eyes that stared directly at her. Vreni suddenly realised she was not invisible to them.

The tear-shaped bottle slipped from her sweating fingers and tumbled in the air. The woman crossed the room in a silent blur and her thin hand wrapped around the glass before it hit the floor. Then she gazed at it and ran a slender finger gently across the glass before placing it back on the shelf.

'Veca Tante.' The words froze in Vreni's mouth even as she spoke them.

The old aunt leaned close, sniffing at Vreni's face. She moved closer again and rubbed her rough cheek against Vreni's, making Vreni think of a cat.

'Another experiment, Rozālija, my love?' the alchemist asked. His eyes sparkled as he looked between Veca Tante and the sleeping girls.

'Not this one, she smells more like food.'

Veca Tante sniffed Vreni again and looked puzzled. She raised her hand to Vreni's face, and ran her papery fingertips across her cheek. Then she flicked her nails. Vreni felt a burning pain and the stinging wetness of blood. Next there was a strange, damp roughness on her face, and Vreni realised the old witch was licking the blood from the scratches she had just made. The woman smacked her lips together, savouring, but then stopped. She stared, bemused, searching Vreni's eyes.

'You taste like something that you cannot be—yet,' she said, shaking her head and licking her thin lips again. 'But you do taste like food, and my little Bruno must be so hungry by now. Would you feed my little Bruno for me?' she asked the alchemist as she walked back to stand by his side.

'Of course, my darling Rozālija,' he said.

Veca Tante leaned in and kissed him lightly on the neck with her bloodstained lips. The alchemist moved towards her, but she raised her hands to stop him. 'Bruno is waiting, and I need to deal with our guard.'

She left the chamber, pulling the door closed behind her.

Vreni could hear the young guard's shaky voice through the door. 'Yes, my lady, I know, but I didn't see her. No, it *will* never happen again.'

The scream entered Vreni's ears like a sharp knife. There was a thump against the other side of the door, and Vreni heard footsteps clicking on the stones, fading down the passage. She felt the remnants of her boiled egg rising from her stomach. She coughed and swallowed hard. *I am responsible for that man's death.*

The alchemist was busying himself unfastening a thick leather belt from around a barrel. He lifted the tattered hide and Vreni could see that it was not a barrel but a circular cage.

Inside the cage was an emaciated wolf, covered with uneven clumps of ragged fur. The creature was circling the cage, and with each turn it looked from the alchemist to Vreni. Its understanding seemed to grow as it circled, and it began to salivate, running its long pink tongue around its ragged mouth. It grinned, showing slick white teeth. The air in the room was pungent with the smell of sweaty fur and rancid drool.

The alchemist hooked a timber lever through a loop in the top of the cage; at the other end of the lever was an empty basket that hung high in the air. 'When the basket fills with grain it will lift Bruno's cage, and you...' He took a knife from his pouch and stabbed a hole in a large sack hanging from the ceiling.

Vreni watched as the grains of rye started flowing out. She heard the door click shut, followed by the heaving *thunk* of the key locking the door.

The wolf was growling, a low and threatening sound, like the rumble of distant thunder. Above the growl came another sound that did not belong. Vreni heard a child's voice. Her eyes flashed to the sleeping girls. Would they be eaten too?

She heard a voice again—no, two voices—coming from near the wolf's cage. She watched the wolf, trying to understand what she was hearing. There couldn't be voices. There was only the wolf circling, but the voices were there and growing louder.

She could see movement beneath the wolf's tattered fur, lumpy swellings growing and rippling beneath its skin. Within the matted tufts of the wolf's fur, little faces pushed through and looked around, blinking. The eyes darted here and there, searching until they saw Vreni, then each one strained, taking turns to watch her as the wolf paced and circled within the cage.

If this is the old woman's pet, what else is she capable of? 'I'll never know now,' Vreni whispered, her voice unsteady.

She was entranced by the confusing horror of this creature and the tiny faces imprisoned within its fur. As the wolf turned in its cage, she could hear the children's voices rise and fall.

'Be careful,' said a singsong voice.

'Don't go into the woods alone,' scolded another.

'You shouldn't stray from the path,' warned a third.

'Say your prayers,' came a fourth.

Together they chorused, 'Run!'

Vreni's heart thundered in her ears. The wolf was pawing at the tiny gap between the stone floor and the bottom of the heavy iron cage.

It couldn't end like this. She wanted to send her birds through to unlock the door, but she looked at the sleeping girls and realised she must protect her sleeping sisters. She reached for the pouch in her pocket and sprinkled the whisper-bird eggs into her palm.

'Torment, anguish, agony,' she whispered. 'The eyes—peck at its eyes.'

The eggs cracked one by one. She saw the wolf's cage lifting up as it forced its muzzle underneath, slavering and biting at the floor trying to wedge its head through the narrow opening.

The minuscule birds stared at Vreni as they ruffled and flapped, growing and growing. The wolf growled and panted, chewing at the stone.

'Don't go into the woods alone,' chanted the entrapped children.

Finally the birds took flight from Vreni's clammy palm. They circled in the stagnant air between Vreni and the wolf.

With a frantic last effort, the wolf pushed under the heavy iron cage and burst out in an unsteady tangle of paws. Its growls were combined with the panicked screams of the tormented children. *How many murders have these wretched young prisoners had to watch over and over again?*

Before the wolf had a chance to turn its attention to her, Vreni dived behind a large wooden bureau that stood in the centre of the room. She heard flapping and chirping. The wolf yelped and growled. It sprang up with its jaws snapping, trying to capture its tormentors and swallow them whole. It leapt about madly, crashing back down to the hard stone floor after each attempt.

Above the tormented clatter, she could hear that the children had started giggling. Then, unbelievably, they started singing.

'Little robin red breast sat upon a tree,
Up went vilks and down went he.
Down came wolfie, and away robin ran.
Says little robin red breast, 'Catch me if you can.'

The birds had formed a cloud of screeching feathers. They circled, taking turns to dive at the wolf, stabbing their sharp beaks into its eyes. Pearls of blood appeared on its mangy face. The wolf continued to snap blindly at its attackers. It yelped and howled in frustration. The captive children giggled and sang, delighted at the creature's anguish.

Vreni unknotted the taming cloth and pulled it from her hips, knowing that this square of fabric was infused with calming herbs and magic. She hoped it would work on this poor, cursed creature. Maybe these were the children the wolf had eaten, and they had come back to torment it. As vile as this creature was, and as tormented as the poor children must be, Vreni knew she could not kill them. She knew they had no more choice about how they were made than Vreni did.

She crept around the cabinet, approaching the wolf from behind. The birds dived and pecked. The children teased and chanted. Vreni threw the flimsy silk cloth onto the wolf's back.

The cloth seemed to wrap itself around the wolf's flanks, and then, with a ripple, it slithered up to cover the animal's shoulders and head, smothering the children's voices. The wolf struggled and growled, trying to free itself from the grip of the cloth. It circled in panic. Small spots of blood began to stain the pale silk. The birds circled quietly above the panting wolf, as though waiting to see if they were still needed.

Slowly the wolf gave up its snarling and collapsed onto the stone floor, its half-starved form looking barely more than a fur-covered skeleton.

The muffled voices of the children had ceased their chanting and were quietly mumbling, 'Good wolfie, good *vilks*.'

With a shaking hand, Vreni reached out and lifted the cloth from the wolf's eyes. It looked at her with sad confusion. 'Veca Tante curses us all in different ways,' she said, as she lightly patted its muzzle with the back of her hand. It whimpered.

She reached for a joint of meat in a box that had been placed close to the wolf's cage where the animal could smell it, but it remained cruelly out of reach. The wolf took the meat gently from her hand and gnawed into it noisily.

The circling birds lifted higher into the chamber, singing cheerfully, and then they found an open window and flew into the sunlit sky, their magic task completed.

Vreni hesitated before slowly lifting the cloth from the wolf's flank. The small faces whose singing had added to the animal's torment were now being pulled back into their horrid prison.

The wolf stopped its chewing for a moment and stared up into Vreni's eyes. It lifted its head so that its face, and teeth, came frighteningly close to hers. She held very still. The wolf nuzzled gently against the wound on her cheek, as if they now shared the pain that Veca Tante had inflicted. They both sighed.

Letting the cloth fall again, she left the wretched creature to feast on the raw, meaty bone and looked again at the young girls lying on the low divan. *What can I do for them? I don't even belong here myself.* All she could do was what she had been asked to do.

She walked away from the girls and picked up the tear-shaped bottle one more time, holding it until the icy menace of the potion inside crept up her arm. She made sure she would remember exactly what it felt like. If it still existed in her world she would now be able to feel its presence and, she hoped, bring it back to the Wise Sisters so the cure could be made.

Vreni took the key for the door from where it hung inside the wolf's cage. She knew she could do nothing about the sleeping girls; she was a visitor and couldn't take anything from this place except wisdom.

A message. She could leave a message for the Sisters to find. *Perhaps the Sisters can save the girls the way they had saved—*

will save—Grandmama and everyone else by softening the curse somehow.

Vreni unlocked the chamber door. The weight of the guard's body pushed the door towards her. There was no visible sign of what had killed him, only thin lines of blood running from his eyes, nose and mouth.

I caused this. She felt the weight of his fate heavy on her shoulders.

She kneeled down beside him and her tears fell on his face. They mixed with his blood as she tried to wipe it with the hem of her dress, as if that would somehow help. 'I'm sorry for what happened to you,' she said. 'Maybe your sacrifice today will make a difference one day.'

She closed his frightened eyes and traced a sign on the dead guard's tunic, and another on the door. If it was the Sisters who attended to the body, she knew they would see the magical message and be guided to find the girls.

With heavy feet Vreni retraced her steps back towards the kitchen, wondering for the first time how she would return home. All at once cries erupted and rippled throughout the palace.

'The Lady Ieva, she is struck down.'

Screaming and weeping followed by the thudding of running feet echoed through the passageways. She followed the commotion to its centre. She saw her grandfather Carls lying with his face pressed against Ieva's death-still body. He was weeping wretchedly, as her mother had done when her father died.

So it has begun.

'My lord, please forgive me,' begged a handmaiden. 'The brooch was a gift; it had just arrived. The lady asked me to pin it on her gown. It was an accident, just a little blood, but now this. I don't understand what's happened.' She sobbed and collapsed to the stony floor. The brooch was pinned to the gown surrounded by a small dark stain of blood. 'I could do nothing.' She crumpled to the floor, shaking.

A woman wearing a spiral pendant, the sign of the Pratigs Māsa, bent over Ieva and spoke privately to Carls. He stared at her with swollen, disbelieving eyes. Then he swiftly scooped his wife up into his arms and followed the woman towards a door at the far end of the vast hall.

Vreni stood and started to thread her way around the edge of the crowd to follow after them. She felt a firm hand on each shoulder.

'This is not your place or time, young sleeper, home you go.'

'But this is my family,' she pleaded.

'This is not your story yet.'

Vreni's two escorts kept a firm grip on her as they walked back through the chaos of the palace towards the bed of straw and rags next to the hearth. As they walked, they started humming gently. Their music surrounded Vreni. She remembered the sleeping girls in the alchemist's chamber.

'Veca Tante has girls, sleepers,' she thought she heard herself say as the two Sisters lay her near the hearth, but the humming voices swam around in her mind and the world of the palace faded from her vision.

Vreni woke with a gasping breath and cried out. 'The girls, they are sleepers, they are trapped. I tried so hard to wake them.' Her words tumbled out. 'I saw Grandmama. I saw it happen. Veca Tante clawed my cheek, she licked me, licked the blood. She was going to feed me to her wolf, and there were children in its fur, singing.' She sobbed bitterly.

Sabina and Anna sat close and held her while they sang. Their song followed on from the one sung by the Sisters who had sent her back from the dream realm. She felt the rhythm of the song taking control and slowing her heartbeat, the soft rise and fall of the music soothing her outrage, and her nightmarish thoughts faded.

'The magic left for me by the Sisters saved me,' she said at last.

'The wolf was cursed to suffer the singing of the children it found lost in the woods and killed,' Anna said. 'We have records of such grotesque, tormented blendings in the *Book of Wisdom*. Veca Tante enjoyed watching the pain of others. She designed magic to lock her victims in an eternal struggle. It wasn't enough to kill them, but the agony made them prefer death. She was filled with so much loathing and desperation that she needed to surround herself with the agony of others.'

'I'm sorry, Vreni,' Sabina said. 'We didn't know of other sleepers, but it stands to reason they would have trialled the potion.'

'So where are they?' Vreni cried. 'Buried? Entombed for all these centuries?' She felt smothered.

'The sleeping girls have you now,' Anna said. 'And they have us. We'll search the ancient records for clues to help us find them.'

It wasn't enough. Vreni wanted the Wise Sisters to find them now. They had slept too long with no one watching over them. No father. No warm, safe bed.

Sabina and Anna began the humming again. They supported Vreni and walked out of the chamber and back up the spiral stairs into a cool night filled with sparkling stars. The moon was high in the sky.

'How long was I—dreaming?' Vreni asked.

'Not long, it's around midnight,' Sabina said.

Only a few hours, but Vreni felt exhausted.

The sisters led her to her room, helped her dress for bed and tucked a soft feather quilt around her.

Sabina rubbed some sweet-smelling oil on her temples and touched the raw red line beginning to raise itself into a scar on the side of Vreni's cheek. 'No more dreams tonight,' she said.

Companion

*We have been observing him. His behaviour
indicates that the glimmer Sabina placed on
him has loosened. He desires understanding
about the glimpses of surfacing knowledge,
and this shows us that he is the one.*

~ Message to Mežs Mājas

Vreni had slept late. When she washed her face next morning, her cheek was stinging and tender. *I might not have returned from the dream realm at all.*

The morning sun flowed over her as she sat at a small table near the window in the dining room. She watched the steam from her tea drift in and out of the beam of sunlight as she slowly peeled away the shell from a boiled egg.

'So, Vreni,' Sabina said, coming to sit opposite her, ' how are you feeling? I hope your cheek's not too painful. We applied ointment last night, and with luck it should heal without a scar. You showed great bravery and skill facing what you did in the dream realm. We feel you're now ready to help us with our ... challenge.'

Vreni's breakfast suddenly tasted sour. Her memories of the dream realm poured over her. She squirmed in her seat.

'I touched the unsoftened potion,' she said. 'I can still feel its blackness clawing towards me through the bottle. Wouldn't my knowledge of that be enough to help you create a remedy? Surely I'd be able to feel something in your new potion that would let you know it would work.'

'We'd be blessed if that were true, Vreni, but no,' Sabina said. 'We still need you to seek out the remaining potion and bring it to us. We can only be successful in reversing the curse completely if we can analyse whatever remains of it. You're the one who can bring it to us.'

'Bring it from where?' Vreni asked.

'The alchemists were forced to flee as we were, but they've continued to conduct their business. They're a corporation now, called AlGuild. Although they're quite secretive and hide themselves away, we also know a lot about hiding so it's hard to stay hidden from us.' Sabina's eyes sparkled. 'Some of their staff can be boastful when they're flattered by a charming woman. We know where their headquarters are, and we're sure that's where they'd keep anything of value to them.'

'So I just go there? Just walk in and feel around for the potion?' Vreni said. 'What makes you so sure about all this?'

'Others have gone there before you,' Sabina said. 'And they found out a lot about the building and the grounds—'

'But they didn't bring back the potion?'

Vreni decided she didn't want to hear the answer. Instead she thought of her mother, Rita and her aunties, held captive by the curse. She remembered her day in the city, seeing normal people with lives that flowed like streams, not frozen ponds, the way hers often seemed to. Finally, she thought of the lost girls, who had no one. The anger and determination she felt last night returned in a flood.

'I'll go to this AlGuild place and search, but am I really ready? How can I manage such a task on my own?'

'You won't be going alone.' Sabina looked towards the door.

As Vreni followed her gaze, Anna walked through the door, followed by a tall male shape silhouetted by the morning sun.

'So where's the dance action around here?'

'William! How—why are you here?' Vreni jumped up and hugged him. He was solid, real.

'Small world,' he said. 'Anna asked me to help with a research project.' He looked around and shrugged. 'Uni likes to send field researchers to build up its reputation, and they also like to get their hands on new research findings first. So I'm here, wherever here is, to help with your work.' He eyed Sabina and Anna questioningly.

'How fortunate that I realised you two seem to know each other,' Anna said from the doorway. 'Please, William, help yourself to some food before we start work. And Vreni, would you give William a tour of our lovely gardens and make him feel welcome? Bring him to the laboratory in about an hour.'

'I'll leave you two to catch up,' Sabina said, following Anna out of the dining room.

'It's great to see you.' William hugged her tight. 'What are you doing here?'

'I'm here studying, too.' Vreni wasn't sure what to say, not knowing how much William remembered.

'How's Rita?' William asked.

'She's about the same. We haven't been doing much. No dancing.'

So much had changed, and Vreni struggled to make small talk. She was glad William hadn't asked about her father, but from what she understood, William's memories of that evening stopped with the dance party. He would have no memory of even being at her house.

She walked over to the breakfast counter and filled a plate for him. 'What are you studying at university?' she asked, even though she knew the answer.

'Science,' he said, getting to work on his breakfast. 'Biochemistry. My father insisted I follow the family tradition. The way he tells it, you'd think our ancestors *invented* chemistry. He's a big corporate hot shot.' William's words seemed tinged with anger. 'But I can't tell you much about him or his work. I've barely seen him over the last few years. He's always working when I'm home, which hasn't been very often, not since I was old enough to be sent away to school. Education is everything to my father. He says that he wants me to join him and work at his company when the time's right. He says it will be an *'irresistible'* offer.

He can be very dramatic. He goes on about how important the work is, but he never tells me anything else.'

'So will you join his company?'

'Not likely.' He pushed his half-empty plate away. 'He's decided everything else for me, but he's not deciding my career path.'

'What about your mother?'

'I never knew her. She died when I was young.'

'That's sad, I'm so sorry,' Vreni said.

'Thanks. It is sad, but I never knew any different. I had a sister as well, she was born two years before I was, but when she was tiny she died in her sleep, you know, SIDS. And just after I was born Mum also died in her sleep. I believe she was unwell after the birth.'

'How horrible.' Vreni reached out and squeezed his hand.

'I was lucky, really, because I was too young to realise. But it must've been unbearable for Dad because he's hardly ever spoken about her. There's not even a photo of her or my sister in the house. It's like they never existed.'

'So he works to fill the space your mother left.'

'Well, something drives him to work all the time, but I'm not like him.'

'In that case, let's take a walk through the gardens before you start work today.' Vreni grabbed William's hand and pulled him out into the warm morning sun.

Because of the old magic used by the Wise Sisters, the grounds surrounding the cottages and the laboratory buildings at Mežs Mājas were kept in a state of perpetual late springtime.

The grass was lush and damp. The trees were thick with leaves and buds, but somehow also loaded with ripening fruit. The moist, cool air was heavy with sweet fragrance, and noisy with the buzz of insects and the song of birds.

Vreni guided William along the gravel paths that wove between the overcrowded garden beds and glinting ponds. When he took hold of her hand she felt a spark, and wondered if he would remember the things that had been hidden by her father and Sabina. But *would it really be fair on him to remember them?*

'This place must have great irrigation because there's nothing but dry scrub for kilometres all around outside the valley,' William said. He seemed to accept this strange place without question.

He stared at her for a long moment, smiled broadly and pulled her off the path.

'Where are we going?' she asked.

'Over there.' He pointed to a small grove of pine trees. 'I heard there was a dance party in there.' He jumped into the clearing at the centre of the grove and started dancing, stomping around like an overwound toy.

Vreni laughed and gave a mocking round of applause.

'Would you like to dance?' he asked, walking over and taking her hand.

Vreni smiled. 'Yes, but just one.'

'We'll see,' William said, pulling her close to him. They stood, swaying together on the spongy carpet of pine needles. He offered a soft kiss, which she accepted.

As they *danced* in each other's arms in the cool shade of the small clearing, Vreni didn't care if he remembered everything or not. He was here with her and that would do for now.

Then William faltered for a moment, tensed slightly and pulled away from her, staring out towards the trees. He wobbled slightly, looking dazed. He shook his head and lowered his gaze to the ground.

'How's *Parvils* doing?' He choked out the question.

Vreni's stomach knotted. 'You remember?'

'Well, I'm not sure. I've had weird, random flashes of things, and that name—I don't know, I thought it was my imagination. The note you pinned to my shirt said you got your driver to take me home because I'd been drinking too much. I didn't remember doing anything except dancing with you. Then all these other things have been flashing up.' William squeezed her hands. 'So I did meet your family?'

'Yes.'

'I remember pieces of a very weird conversation, but I don't remember getting home, so for a while I believed your note.'

'The conversation was real, and weird,' she said. 'My father and Artūrs, our driver, gave you drinks that made you forget and fall asleep. Then Artūrs drove you home.'

'So the sleeping-curse thing is real?'

Heat rose in Vreni's face. 'It's real.'

William lurched and leaned against a tree, then slid down the trunk and landed heavily at the base. He stared at the ground, shaking his head. 'How is Rita, really?' he said.

'She's still sleeping, and safe, because of you.'

'When will she wake up?'

'Whenever she does. We never know how long we'll sleep.' Vreni shrugged. 'We just wait.'

'Unbelievable. How could that possibly happen?'

'You heard the *fairytale* my father told you that night. Trust me, it's true. I'm proof,' she said, spreading her arms out wide. 'Ta-da.'

William shook his head again, shrugged and then smiled. 'How is Parvils? And what was in those drinks?'

Vreni felt herself sag. Her knees buckled, and William reached and caught her. She sat next to him, feeling the roughness of the tree's trunk through her shirt. 'Papa died.'

Each time she said the words, it became more real. Her throat ached and wouldn't let her say more. William wrapped his arms around her and waited.

'He was very old,' she began in a whisper. 'The Wise Sisters in Papa's tale have magic that can extend life, but no one outlives a sleeper. You already know that our lives span centuries. We leave so much behind us because we're trapped in the cycles of long-sleep. Papa waited, and protected us while we slept, and now he's been left behind by us.'

Vreni leaned into the warmth of William's chest and cried quietly. Surrounded by the cool freshness of the pine grove, she told him about the other astounding things that had happened since she arrived at Mežs Mājas.

'What an amazing world I've danced my way into,' he joked, kissing her lightly on the forehead.

'Speaking of amazing, you seem *amazingly* okay with all the things you've found out. You must have a high strangeness threshold.'

'Honestly, Vreni, I don't know. Maybe I don't believe it all yet, maybe I just wanted to hear you out, to hear the whole story.' He nodded slowly. 'The scientific, logical me wants proof, but the dancing me is fascinated by it all. And I'm fascinated by you too, of course,' he added dramatically.

'Of course,' Vreni joined in. 'Maybe you're under my spell.' Her father said that the Wise Sisters saw something in William. Or had they done something to him, something they hadn't told her about yet? The sisters were good at secrets.

Sabina appeared, walking towards the grove of pines. William fell silent in mid-sentence, looking awkward.

'She's a sister, William, she knows it all.' Vreni gestured to Sabina. 'The Pratigs Māsa—the Wise Sisters—are part of my family's support, part of the circle of influence Papa talked to you about that night.'

'So am I really here to do research?' William asked.

'Do you want him to go with me?' Vreni asked Sabina and shook her head. 'This is not William's problem.' But she couldn't help thinking how much she wanted him to be there with her. First date: steal a body. Second date: unknown danger. *Maybe I'll never be a good girlfriend to have.*

'Go where?' William asked.

'Yes, if he's willing we'll send him with you,' Sabina confirmed.

'But it'll be dangerous,' Vreni protested.

'What will be dangerous?' he asked.

'There have been previous attempts,' Sabina said, 'and because of those efforts we're better prepared now. Your glimmer is gone. Look inside yourself, at the training, the magic. You'll see how truly ready you are, *Sister Veronika*.'

'What?' William asked loudly. He stood up. 'What? Where? What danger? I'm right here, you know.'

'I'm sorry, William, everything will be made clear soon,' Sabina said. 'For now, know that you will play a vital part in this. I need to show you both what we know, but let's talk more inside.'

Plans Within Plans

~ Mežs Mājas, strategy discussions

The laboratory was clean and white and ordered. A few sisters were working quietly on something that looked surprisingly uninteresting to Vreni, considering how magical everything else had been so far. The lab workers nodded towards them as they followed Sabina past the benches and through a heavy stained-glass door at the end of the lab.

The room behind the door was vastly different. At its centre was a broad wooden table covered with antiquated bottles and bowls, and lush bunches of herbs that filled the air with a sweet, spicy aroma.

Anna sat stiffly at the table studying the yellowing pages in a heavy, leather-bound book. Sabina indicated that they should sit.

Vreni glanced at the book's mottled pages; she could see by the changes of penmanship that the text must have been written by many sisters over the years. The pages were peppered with diagrams, runes and colourful illuminations. Anna turned the page and Vreni saw a highly decorated drawing of a labyrinth.

Anna looked up from the book. 'So are you two willing to help us?'

'Help you do *what*?' William's voice had an edge now.

'To help us free Vreni's family from the sleeping curse once and forever,' Anna said.

William started to speak, but Anna raised her hand to stop him and continued. 'We've travelled and hidden alongside their family throughout the centuries, and we've watched as the Alķimķi Ģilde also manoeuvred and concealed themselves. We know they've continued to grow their riches and power. They've become the AlGuild, and, like us, they've developed a necessary corporate structure to continue their true purpose.'

Anna rubbed her hand thoughtfully over the painted illumination of the labyrinth. 'We need you two to enter the AlGuild compound and retrieve what remains of the original sleeping potion. Over the years we've studied and developed our knowledge. All we need now is the last remnant of the potion and we can fully reverse its effects and free you all.'

William tried to joke. 'Happily ever after.'

'Yes, but without the *ever*,' Vreni said. 'Our family's had more than its fair share of *everafter* already.'

Anna continued, ignoring their attempt at banter. 'We believe the AlGuild would keep anything they prize inside a remote centre for research and development. It wouldn't do their corporate image any good if people discovered their true nature, or their grisly history. You saw some of that, Vreni, in the dream realm, and you need to know they haven't changed much over the centuries. AIGuild continues to profit from destruction and misery, and we, through our holdings, endeavour to diminish and soften the harm they do to people and the environment.'

Anna glanced at Sabina, who continued. 'We've learned from previous attempts that the internal layout of the R&D building is in the form of a labyrinth. If this holds to the labyrinth of legend, you'll find what you seek in its centre. There's only one path in, and if they're true to the legend there'll be a shorter, direct path out.' Sabina smiled weakly at Anna.

'A labyrinth is not a maze, one path in and one path out,' Vreni said. 'So why have you failed before?'

'It's true that there's no choice but to follow the single labyrinthine path,' Anna said. 'The labyrinth is like life, and in life we sometimes face—challenges along the way.'

'You'll do well against these challenges, Vreni,' Sabina said. 'We know. We watched you in the dream realm.'

'Watched? How?' Vreni asked, amazed.

'Mention of you is in here.' Anna patted the book. 'There's a story of a girl that fits your description, who came and went on the day of the cursing. The sisters took note because this girl knew where to find the box of spells, and how to use the magic it contained without needing any instructions.'

'We sent you to the dream realm already knowing you would be successful,' Sabina said.

'But I'll be travelling in the real world now,' Vreni said.

'The dream realm was real enough while you were there,' Sabina said, touching the scar on Vreni's cheek. 'And you used your magic with skill and bravery.' She took both of Vreni's hands in hers. 'Have faith, Sister Veronika, bringer of victory,' she said formally.

'So if I'm going to be victorious why does William have to come with me?'

'To enter the main building there's a bio-lock, a touch pad,' Sabina explained. 'We've created an amulet, a key, that allows the wearer to open the door, but if *you* touch the panel, Vreni, the system will sense the magic in you and you won't even get inside. William will open the door for you.' She placed a silver, key-shaped amulet around his neck.

'The compound is fenced but not guarded,' Anna said. 'They've created elemental pets, like the wolf you saw in the dream realm, to defend the grounds around the building. We don't know what these defences will be because these pets tend to destroy themselves or each other frequently and new ones replace them. We just know what we've seen in the past.'

'We also know that the members of AIGuild are complacent,' Sabina continued. 'They presume their defences will kill any intruders so they don't monitor the grounds in any other way. They won't be expecting anyone to survive the trip through their Pleasure Gardens and come picking their bio-lock.'

'If they follow with traditions about labyrinths laid down in the ancient myths, once you're inside you'll meet these *challenges* as you move through the building,' Anna said. 'We're making every preparation possible to support you. You'll have William, but we'll be with you as well, in our own way.'

Anna looked at Sabina and tilted her head questioningly. Sabina widened her eyes and gave the slightest shake of her head in return.

'We're making final preparations tonight,' was all Anna said.

'All will become clear for you both in the morning. Go and rest. Spend some time together. I'm so glad you've found each other again.' Sabina squeezed Vreni and William's hands, and smiled. 'Go, we'll see you both tomorrow.'

—⚏—

The evening was cool and quiet in the garden. The daytime frenzy of bees and birds had given over to the slow, regular sound of some unseen insect that thrummed quietly to welcome the rising moon.

Vreni and William found a shadowy, hidden place that was separated from the rest of the garden by a tall curving hedge. They sat on a smooth polished bench; the wood still held the last of the day's warmth. The black glass of the pond mirrored the golden light that spilled from the cottage windows and into the darkness. Laughter and chatter rose and fell.

They sat for a long moment, held by the evening calm.

'Are you sure you want to do this?' Vreni asked quietly.

'It could be the start of something beautiful between us,' William said in a mock-romantic voice.

Vreni realised that he wasn't going to be serious about what lay ahead, not tonight, so she joined in with his joke. 'Maybe you're a little too old to be my boyfriend,' she teased. 'You're at university already.'

William burst out laughing. '*I* am too old for *you*?' he snorted. 'If my estimations are correct, I won't be too old to be your *boyfriend* for approximately eighty-two more years. You look great for your age, by the way. And what is that, one hundred and how many?'

She punched him. He kissed her and everything else faded; there was only the kiss. She rested her head on his shoulder, remembering all the details of all their kisses, and locking the happy thrill of them safely in her heart so she would have them forever.

'So you just freeze in time during long-sleep?' he said quietly after a while.

'That's what happens; everything stops.'

'You must've seen so many changes in one hundred years,' William said.

'I suppose that's something good about the curse, I've seen some amazing things. If people had said that such things were possible back when I was young we would've questioned their sanity, and now I've seen more than I could ever have imagined.'

'It must be like having a time machine.'

She smiled. 'I suppose so. When I was young it was still mostly horses for travel and fire for cooking, especially in the countryside. Since then I've seen cars appear and reinvent themselves, getting sleeker and faster with each awakening. I've seen television and telephone. What marvels they are, where sound and images can be sent along wires, through the air, to be shared by thousands, and now millions. I remember being terrified when I first saw planes roaring through the sky, and even more amazingly, the next time I woke humans had ripped themselves free of Earth and sent men all the way to the moon. I watched it, you know, I watched *my* Neil Armstrong walk on the moon.' She sighed.

'Oh, *my* astronaut hero,' William said, putting his hands over his heart.

'Ooh, jealous,' she teased. 'You know, I vowed I would go there one day, and with all the fantastic things that had already happened I thought it would just be a matter of time, but I'm still waiting. Maybe one day. Computers are the most astounding things of all, but they gave Papa lots more excuses to make us stay at home. He said we could shop online and see any place on Earth at the click of a button.'

'So you all just sleep and wake and —' He shrugged.

'It's the way it's always been for me. Sometimes Rita's awake, sometimes Mama, sometimes all of us together, even my aunties. Sometimes Rita is older than me,' she laughed. 'Now, that can feel strange. But I guess nothing will seem strange ever again after tomorrow. That will be—'

'What about all the magic?' he interrupted before she could finish. Where does that fit in?'

'Grandmama had many aunts—Magrietina, Dālija, Lilija, Efeja and Rozālija, that was Veca Tante's name. They were the original Wise Sisters. They spun the old magic. Grandmama inherited everything instead of Rozālija, so the old aunt became filled with envy and hatred, and she looked for the darkness in the magic, fear instead of faith, cruelty instead of love, and death instead of life. She wove death, spun it into a potion—you know the rest.'

'This AlGuild is really still operating after all this time? What about this Veca Tante, could she still be alive?'

'Maybe. Rita and I wonder about that sometimes. Her sisters used magic to extend their lives, but I doubt any magic would work for four centuries.'

'And you? You're quite beautiful for an *old* lady.'

'That's because I get plenty of beauty sleep.' She nudged him hard in the ribs with her elbow. She stood up, leaned down and kissed him. 'Speaking of sleep ...'

She took his hand and led him to the small gardener's cottage that had been prepared for him. Then she kissed his cheek and turned for her own bed, drawn by the echoing lilt of the Sisters' voices as they filled the evening air with the sound of their humming.

Amulets

*William has responded well to the recovery of
the hidden memories we folded into his glimmer.
His allegiance appears strong. Our suspicions
and hopes about him have proven correct. He
is the key. He's the one to breach the door to
the labyrinth. He may falter when he learns
his lineage, but I feel the goodness in his heart.
Others might presume his fate is predestined,
but we all have freewill. We will proceed.*

~ Anna and Sabina, strategy planning

Early-morning sunlight sliced through the violet shadows within Vreni's room. The brightness penetrated her eyelids and blended with her dream of the cool garden the evening before, where she had sat with William. In the dream the moonlight dappled her face, but the moonlit dream was gradually solidifying into day, the day she would walk into AlGuild.

Her hands tightened into fists. She was fully awake.

When Vreni reached the dining room, William was already sitting in a block of bright sunlight at the table by the window.

He was picking curiously at a platter of blackbread, cheeses and fruit-filled pastries.

She realised her hands were clenched again and she made a conscious effort to relax them. *Whatever this day brings, it will happen soon enough without me talking about it now.* She crossed the room, hoping that William would be pretending too.

'I could ask the kitchen if they have porridge instead.' She lightly kissed the top of his head.

'No, no, I'm just glad you're here. I was wondering if I was expected to eat all this myself.'

'Of course it's all for you,' she joked, 'and lots of coffee to wash it down.' She poured two cups of coffee and put one in front of him. '*Ēst! Baudīt!*' She gestured dramatically towards the platter. 'Eat! Enjoy!'

'I heard you mention porridge,' the cook said, placing a large, steaming bowl on the table.

'Thank you,' they both said, laughing.

'Don't mention any more food,' William whispered, ' or we'll be here until lunch.'

'Shhh, don't say *lunch*,' she whispered, laughing.

After a breakfast filled with fake small talk, they walked slowly through the gardens towards the lab building. Vreni remained silent, not trusting herself to talk about what might be coming soon. She didn't want to hear what

William might say in reply. She knew everything would change once they went inside.

The lab door squeaked open. They nodded polite greetings as they walked past the Sisters, who looked as though they'd been sitting at the workbenches since yesterday.

Vreni walked slowly to the other end of the sterile white room, looking at the stained-glass birds and flowers that were all that was left between her and this day starting. She breathed deeply and pushed open the heavy door.

Inside, she was surprised to see that Sabina and Anna were not sitting at the table. Instead, an ancient Sister sat there, reading and scribbling notes. The old woman stopped and looked up at them as they entered. Her piercing blue eyes stared out through folds of papery skin. Without introducing herself, she started speaking as if William and Vreni had only stepped out of the room a moment ago.

'We're as sure as we can be that the AIGuild building conceals a labyrinth.' She was drawing a labyrinth on a small scrap of paper as she spoke. 'Because the path through the labyrinth winds around on itself, wheels within wheels, the passageways fold, wrapping around each other, offering maximum protection to whatever is at its centre. So the centre is where you need to go.' She began tracing a path on her drawing with her crooked finger. 'There's only ever one path to the centre of a labyrinth, so there can be no shortcuts and the way will be defended.'

She looked up. 'You have visited the dream realm, Veronika. You've seen a small example of AIGuild's beginnings. You have firsthand knowledge of what they're capable of. We can't predict what might await you once you enter the labyrinth, but we'll be with you. All the Wise Sisters here at Mežs Mājas have gathered what they need from the earth and the animals to form magical charms and amulets that hold the power of nature within them, ready for you to bring to life, to do your bidding as you see fit. Along with this nature magic, the Sisters have stored magic from themselves, which they give freely as their contribution to your quest.'

Vreni shook her head. 'I don't understand.'

'Remember the talismans and charms you discovered hidden in your clothes that gave you protection? You'll wear something similar but many times more powerful.'

The old Sister reached for an ornate box on the table. She lifted the lid and gently removed a thick ribbon of silk that was knotted to form a large crimson loop. Threaded onto the ribbon was a cluster of small glass spheres that glinted, reflecting the soft light of the desk lamp. She laid them gently in the palm of her creased hand.

Vreni leaned in to look more closely at the necklace. The spheres contained whirling colours and what appeared to be tiny objects. She tried to see inside the glass balls. Some were filled with what looked like coloured smoke or mist, swirling and twisting as if it were alive and straining to be free of its glass prison. Others seemed to contain liquids.

Some of the liquids were transparent and others appeared to have tiny particles floating in them. Two of the spheres shone like pearls, one golden and the other cool silver.

'The magic ... the charms on this necklace hold the tools you might need to complete this journey, young Sister Veronika, but they're only tools. You'll need to use your powers to realise the potential within each sphere. It'll be up to you how and when you use them. They will obey you. Your intentions will become their undeniable purpose.'

'But how will I—' Vreni's question was cut short.

'You will know, Veronika. Reflect on the lessons you discovered when we lifted the glimmer. That was a lifetime of training for you, and a century of careful preparation by us. You are the one, look inside and see that it's true.' The old Sister grasped Vreni's hands and locked her in an icy stare. She drew closer and began humming quietly.

Vreni leaned heavily on the edge of the table as felt the old woman somehow visiting her thoughts. The memories of her training began shifting around inside her mind, flashing vividly as she was guided to recall them all. With each rising memory, Vreni felt the strength of the magical influence build within her. She felt sure this ancient Sister was adding her own strength to Vreni's skill.

The old woman finally released Vreni's hands from her grip and smiled.

'Thank you for reminding me,' Vreni said, as she caught her breath and reached towards the necklace.

The old Sister's eyes sparkled within the soft folds of her smile and she placed the necklace into Vreni's hands. 'The green liquid in this charm is the softening formula we used to save your grandmother.' She touched the gold and silver pearls, and a third, which was blood red. 'The silver one is filled with the powerful chanting of your Sisters, and the gold is their glorious singing. Never forget how powerful our words are. The red one is filled with the strength of all the Sisters here today.'

'And these?' Vreni asked, touching the spheres that seemed to contain something alive.

'All of these ones are full of things that wiggle and squirm and fly and hop,' the Sister said. 'Nature's creatures ready to do your bidding.'

Vreni thought of the whisper birds; they were such tiny creatures, but they were still able to defend her against the wolf.

She cast her eye across the other charms. They created an amazing glistening rainbow, but her eyes were drawn to the two spheres that hung in the very centre of the cluster. One contained a bright turquoise-blue eye that stared out knowingly at her, and inside the other was a pair of rosy, disembodied lips that looked to be drawn into a sad smile.

'These ones are different,' Vreni said.

'With those charms you'll never be alone,' the crinkled face answered.

Alone. Vreni felt dizzy and cold. 'Where are Sabina and Anna?' she asked.

'They are preparing.' The old Sister took the string of charms from Vreni and touched them gently. 'It's time for you to go to them and complete final arrangements before you leave.'

The old woman stood with surprising agility and placed the loop of silken ribbon holding the amulets around Vreni's neck. Then she gripped her shoulders, smiled at her warmly and kissed her on the forehead with her soft, wrinkled lips. Without saying anything more, she turned and pushed open the door behind the table and walked through, leaving Vreni and William to follow.

In the adjoining room the air was filled with singing and chatter and the Sisters moved purposefully to and fro. Details about the room seeped into Vreni's awareness. First, the singing and chanting was too quiet for the number of sisters present, and a group stood motionless at the edge of the room, fixed in a trance-like state, holding bowls and baskets full of insects and animals.

Sabina and Anna were still nowhere to be seen. Why weren't they here preparing with everyone else? Her breath quickened as she searched the room for them again.

'Tell me what they're doing,' Vreni said to the old Sister, walking towards the group of entranced Sisters who were holding equally spellbound creatures.

'Those amulets you're wearing all need physical substance to work,' the old woman said. 'We took the creatures and placed them within the charm you're wearing. These Sisters stay here giving their comfort, calmness and resolve to each remaining insect and animal in their group. The Sisters will stay with them like this, not eating, drinking or sleeping until your task is done. By doing this we're offering one of our Sisters to take the place of the missing members of their swarm, or army, or flutter. It's the exchange we make for their sacrifice.'

'And the silent singers?' Vreni stared at the group of swaying Sisters. They appeared to be singing but they made no sound.

'You have amulets, the gold and silver pearls that contain the powerful songs and chants we have used in our magic for centuries, so of course these singers have given their voices,' the old Sister said, smiling.

'But they can't give up so much for me.' Vreni's eyes burned with tears.

'Calm yourself, young Sister Veronika. They're fully committed to this cause, and their sacrifice is only temporary. All will return to normal at the end of your quest.'

'But what if I don't—'

'Hush, girl, the balance will always be restored in its own way.' The old woman gently wiped a lone tear from Vreni's cheek.

All at once Vreni's resolve crumbled. Her breakfast started churning in her stomach. She let out a long sigh, as if she was deflating, and crouched down close to the cool stone floor. 'Where are Sabina and Anna? I can't do this alone,' she whispered.

William leaned down and gently helped her stand.

'You're never alone, Sister Veronika,' the old Sister said. 'Look around you. You have the talent, magic and love of all the Wise Sisters with you always. You have William bearing the magic of the key, and our magic will ensure that Sabina's eyes will see what you see, and that the words from Anna's lips will guide you and advise you on your journey through the labyrinth.'

'What does that mean? Where are they?' Vreni felt hot. Her stomach was a storm. She searched the room, willing Sabina and Anna to appear and comfort her.

Finally, she saw them enter. As they came closer, and Vreni could see their faces, the meaning of the old Sister's words became frighteningly clear. One of Sabina's eyes was gone. Where her right eye should be, smooth, pale skin had grown over as though the eye had never been there. All that remained was a hollow covered with taut skin, framed by a curved line of long dark eyelashes. The eyelid appeared to be sealed closed, covering the empty socket where her eye used to be.

Next to Sabina was the unbelievable sight of Anna. Yesterday, Anna had had a serene smile and a mouth always full of song and wise words, but today there was nothing but a tiny, shrivelled fissure where her lips used to be.

Vreni heard a sobbing groan rise in her throat. Sabina and Anna held their arms open, and she ran and hugged them.

'Why have you done this thing?' Vreni said with a trembling voice.

'Because we promised to be with you, just as the aunts promised to be with your grandmother centuries ago,'

Sabina said, 'and it's these promises that makes the Wise Sisters stronger with each challenge we face. We will travel with you through our amulets. We want to be with you.'

And we want to keep an eye on you two lovebirds.

Vreni gasped. Anna's voice came from somewhere inside her own head. She placed her hands to her temples and looked at Anna, whose eyes were smiling even if what was left of her mouth could not.

'She can speak with you and answer your questions,' Sabina explained quietly.

'But how will you hear what I say?' Vreni looked among the charms and saw a tiny ear. 'Oh no!' She quickly ran her hands across Sabina's cheeks and under her long, dark hair, and felt an unnatural smoothness where her right ear should have been. 'I can't ask you to do this thing. Undo it now,' she begged.

'Hush,' whispered Sabina, holding Vreni close. 'This is my choice. I—we—want to be with you.' Sabina stared at her. The sealed eye twitched as she smiled. 'I will serve as the eyes and ears of your Sisters, to watch out for you, and Anna will relay our messages and be your advisor along the journey.'

They each took one of Vreni's hands. 'The Wise Sisters are never alone,' Sabina said reassuringly.

Vreni felt the enormous weight of the amulets she was wearing. Her Sisters had made unthinkable sacrifices to aid her on this quest. Their faith was their true gift to her. They believed she was Sister Veronika, bringer of victory.

They believed she would bring the potion to them, and when she did, their faith would be rewarded, and they would all be restored and made whole again.

The Wise Sisters had lived with this *lore* throughout the centuries. They knew that for someone to achieve a thing they needed to be willing to sacrifice something towards that achievement. *I hope I can repay their sacrifice.*

'William, you have your amulet,' Sabina said, touching the key-shaped charm that hung around his neck. 'When you reach the door of the building, hold this with one hand before you place your other hand on the bio-lock pad. We'll try to get you as close as we can to the boundary fence at the south side of the AlGuild compound, but you have to travel through the surrounding grounds by yourselves. As we told you, they're defended but not guarded. Though these defences will be dangerous enough, you only need concern yourself with overcoming them, as the only guard we've seen is at the building's front door. If he doesn't see you, there won't be anyone else outside the building to raise the alarm.'

Three of the young Sisters came in and mumbled their blessings. Sofia gave Vreni her favourite scarf, and William his coat. Emma offered a small bundle, which William stowed in an inside coat pocket.

'Bring the potion back in this,' Emma said, handing Vreni a small pouch on a silk ribbon.

Vreni linked arms with Sabina and Anna as they made their way back through the lab and out into the morning sunshine. They crunched reluctantly across the gravel path, and after forcing cheerful goodbyes and good-lucks Vreni and William slid into the back seat of the car and drove away.

The Pleasure Gardens

*AlGuild has power over nature and the
elements, as we do, but they only achieve
destruction. Their pets wait within the grounds
of the compound, and defend it as their form
and nature permits. AlGuild is satisfied and
complacent, and posts only one human guard.*

~ Pratigs Māsa, quest records

Vreni and William landed lightly on the grass inside the high but otherwise undefended fence that surrounded the AlGuild compound. They looked around cautiously. There were no guards in sight.

Vreni heard Anna's disembodied voice: *The fence doesn't need to be a barrier. You haven't met the real defences yet.*

To the north, the flat steel roof of the imposing AlGuild building was just visible behind a grass-covered ring of mounded earth. East of the building, they could see the security gate, which was closed and unattended. A pathway ran from the deserted carpark outside the gate through a break in the miniature hills. They guessed the path led towards the building's entrance.

They walked east for a short distance along the fence line, then turned and walked west again, trying to decide how to approach. It would have been reassuring to have satellite photos of the compound but, not surprisingly, the Sisters had not been able to find any.

The gardens were vast and quiet. The building and its one human guard were a long way off, but they didn't know who or what would be guarding the door. Vreni thought of the wolf in the dream realm and shuddered.

'I wonder what they use for defence out here,' she said.

'I guess we'll know soon enough,' William replied.

Walking northward towards the raised, grassy ring, they had taken no more than a dozen steps when a strong wind blew up from the north with such force that they had to lean into it to keep moving at all.

'Their defence is to blow us back over d'fence,' William joked. He took Vreni by the hand and together they pushed into the now howling wind.

Vreni could see a faint stain gathering in the air above the ring of low hills. It seemed to hover, as if waiting, preparing itself. She looked on, captivated, wanting to keep watching even though she knew it indicated nothing good.

The distant, stained air coalesced into a small dark tornado. The funnel took on a solid shape and then started moving south, not on a random path as might be expected, but aiming directly at them.

'They do mean to blow us back over the fence,' she said, tightening her grip on William's hand.

As the outer edge of the tornado reached them, they felt the sting of dust and dirt that was being blown around by the wind. The particles gave the swirling funnel a red-brown colour. Small pebbles and tiny sharp fragments stung the skin on their face and arms.

Suddenly they were inside the tornado. It howled and screamed around them. Vreni closed her eyes tightly. She could feel needle-like shards stabbing at her eyelids as if they were trying to reach her eyes and blind her. Her nostrils filled with dust. The dust smelled of blood. She wondered if this dust had mixed with the blood of others who had failed to breech the AIGuild's defences.

William and Vreni clung to each other. They could no longer see which way they should be walking or what other dangers might be hiding inside the dark screeching vortex.

The shards were larger now, and sharper. They were digging into their skin, cutting them. Vreni felt an unexpected coolness on her skin as the wind blew over it, and she realised her blood was being cooled by the menacing wind.

She felt an abrupt coldness, and her mind was suddenly bombarded with images of battered bodies spinning around, being twisted and contorted by the wind. She tried to open her eyes but the red dust blasted at them. She tried to push away the vision of horror, but failed, and she stood frozen.

The images in her mind were of bodies tumbling endlessly, ragged flesh being shredded, and droplets of blood being blown away by the unceasing gale; arms and legs being pulled and snapped, the flesh stripped from their bodies until there was nothing left except pieces of bone worn down into tiny chunks of rubble; tiny sharpened needles that sliced and ripped and whirled in the frenzy. She imagined piles of bones, polished clean and left lying in the tornado's wake, shining in the sunshine as the only remnant of the tornado's passing.

She was drawn from this ghostly vision by the pain of sharp objects that pelted her rigid body. She realised with a shudder that the tornado had given her a view of their fate. They were to become what she had seen: mashed flesh and broken bone.

William leaned heavily against her. He was pulling down on her arm, on her shoulder. She thought he must be so badly hurt that he could no longer *stand*. Her knees buckled under his weight and she fell onto the grass. He was pressing into her back with his hand, pushing her down. He didn't stop until she lay flat on the ground.

She noticed the sweet smell of the grass for a brief moment and then she felt the great weight of William lying on top of her, his arms encircling her face. The screech of the wind lessened slightly as his arms blocked the noise. She realised that William wasn't injured; he was protecting her.

They lay together as the bloody storm raged around them. Within the howls of the wind Vreni was sure she heard screams, voices crying out in anguish. She wanted to raise her head because she was so sure she would be able to see the tortured faces, but William held her down too firmly. The screams pushed their way into her mind until she wanted to jump up and join in their tortured howling, but she remained on the ground, and at last the screams and the faces faded.

Everything became still. The wind had stopped even more quickly than it had started, and the silence buzzed in her ears.

'Vreni, stay down, it's just the eye of the tornado,' William said.

She struggled free of his protective arms for long enough to see the red wall of the spinning funnel surrounding them and a tiny circle of blue sky far above. She felt for the necklace, making sure the charms were there and wondering what action she should take.

She heard Anna's voice: *No, Veronika, no magic, not out here. If they don't see evidence of magic they'll assume their pets have dealt with the problem and they won't even come and look. Wind is just breath; we can only breathe out for so long. It will exhaust itself soon enough.*

'Anna says it will end soon,' she said to William.

'But not until—'

His words were lost as the gritty winds started to lash them again. He pushed her face down into the grass again and covered her. She could feel his body tensing as the chunks of bone struck him. They lay huddled together, faces pushed into the ground, listening to the howling wind. At first Vreni cringed every time she felt William's body tense and flinch, but as the onslaught continued his recoiling gave her comfort.

If he was reacting, he was alive. She was not going to be left alone … yet.

—⁘—

Anna was right. The wind did finally blow itself out. Finally they dared to raise their heads, and then rolled over and lay on the grass staring up at the peaceful blue of the sky. There was no sign of the maelstrom except for a circle of flattened, blood stained grass where the tornado had touched down.

Vreni's face felt stiff, as if she was wearing a mask. When she moved her mouth to speak her face stung, her skin felt as though it had been burned, and she could see bruises already forming where her arms had been struck with pieces of bone.

William's face was smeared with red, and his coat was tattered and ripped. Vreni thought of the shredded bodies she had seen in her vision and knew it could have been much worse.

'We could've been ripped to shreds,' William said, helping her sit up.

'That's what I saw, in some kind of vision,' she said. 'I saw the others, the ones who've already died inside that storm.'

'I saw some of them, too, like some kind of hallucination. Interesting strategy using the visions so we'd stand, frozen with fear, while the tornado ripped us to pieces. It didn't work, though.'

'No, but that was because of you. I was overwhelmed, but you could still think, still act. Thank you.'

'You're welcome.' He shrugged and brushed the dust off his coat sleeves. 'It makes sense that you're more sensitive to it, with all that *magicky* stuff you do.'

'Magicky?'

They stood slowly and checked themselves for any injuries before heading north again.

The ring of mounded earth now blocked their view so they moved cautiously through a low point to check what lay ahead. Within the ring of hills was a wide band of manicured lawn, bordered on the far side by an equally broad ring of flowers, and beyond that a ring of trees, and beyond the trees the building, almost fully hidden.

The circle of lawn curved away in both directions, as did the hills. Midway across the ring of neat green lawn was a series of ponds, spaced evenly around what could be seen of the grass circle. Each pond was decorated with a few glass statues that had been placed at the water's edge.

'It seems oddly unnecessary to have statues here where no one will see them,' Vreni said, staring at the nearest pond. All she could think about was the cool water— washing off the blood and dust, and cooling down her burning skin. She stepped forward.

'Wait,' cautioned William, grabbing her arm.

'What, sea monsters?'

She shook off his hand and kept walking. She kneeled at the edge of the pond and scooped up handfuls of cool water and splashed her face, then rinsed the red crust from her arms. She kicked off her boots and socks and plunged her feet into the water. She laughed at William, who was standing back from the pond as if he was on guard duty.

'You look like a gypsy,' she teased. She took her scarf, wet it in the pond and threw the wet ball of cloth at him. 'Wash off the dust.'

William caught the wet scarf and sat down, wiping red grime from his face and hands. Vreni lay back on the grass and closed her eyes. She would take advantage of William guarding her for just a moment and rest. The water felt cool on her feet. It felt almost too cool and she felt a chill seeping into her bones.

'Come on, Sleeping Beauty, it's time to get going,' William called.

'I know.' Vreni pulled her feet out of the water and stood up. 'My feet feel frozen anyway.' She laughed and reached for her boots, but as she went to take a step she found that her feet would not move; it was as if they were planted in the ground.

'William!' She lost her balance and fell over.

William was by her side in a second. Gelatinous ribbons of water trailed up from the pond's surface, reaching out of the pond and wrapping around Vreni's feet and ankles. He looked at the strange unfrozen ice holding her prisoner and then at the icy crystal statues standing around the pond.

'No way!'

'What is it?'

'Another defence,' was all he said.

'But I can't move.'

William ran to the pond's edge and grabbed a large rock. He lifted it high into the air.

'What are you doing?' she cried.

He didn't wait to answer but brought the rock down with full force onto the ribbons of crystallising water on her feet. They shattered, became liquid again and splashed onto the grass.

'Move!' he yelled, pulling her away from the pond.

Vreni stumbled and had trouble standing. William held her, bearing her weight, and forced himself to look at her feet.

'What was all that about?' she asked, stifling a sob.

'Did I hurt you?'

'I don't think so,' she said, wriggling her toes.

'Thank goodness. I hoped I'd broken the crystal and not your feet.' He hugged her.

'What—'

'The water from the pond was hardening around your feet,' he explained.

'You mean those statues are —' She groped for her boots and scuttled further away from the water.

'Yep, victims of the second defence,' he said. He supported her as she tried to calm her shaking legs.

'Earth and water,' Vreni said. 'The defences out here are created from the elements.'

'Earth—well, dirt and bone—swirling at lethal speeds inside a tornado, and water that freezes you into a crystal statue.' William shuddered.

'Only air and fire to go,' Vreni said, pulling on her boots.

'Only,' William said quietly, handing back her scarf.

—◊—

Everything remained still and quiet in the garden. So far Sabina and Anna's theory had been proven right; the defence system seemed to work independently of any guards, and there was no sign they had been noticed yet. They kept walking steadily northward. They watched and listened, alert for the next elemental defence.

'Fire is obviously dangerous, but at least we'll see it coming,' William said.

'We can't see air, but I don't know how air could be dangerous,' Vreni said.

They walked cautiously across the last of the neat green lawn. The next ring of the garden was filled with wildflowers, scattered randomly among a shaggy carpet of green. Long, spindly stalks supported swollen yellow-green flower buds. Some of the flowers were open, dotting the waving sea of green with bright colour.

Beyond the wildflowers Vreni could see a circle of trees planted close together to create a dense shady arbour, and beyond the treetops she saw glimpses of the AlGuild building.

The labyrinth was inside. Would the potion really be there? What else would they find? But they weren't there yet, so she focused again on the flowers, watching for any sign of danger.

William led the way into the wildflowers. Up close, the buds looked like swollen, misshapen tulips, balanced on top of over-tall stems that were green-brown and thorny. The blooms swayed in the light breeze.

Vreni heard Anna's voice: *Do you still have your knife?*

'Yes.' Vreni touched the smooth leather handle of the knife hanging at her hip.

Good, you'll need it soon.

'Why?' Vreni gripped the handle, and her hand was suddenly clammy. She scanned the sea of flowers again. Nothing. 'Why?' she repeated.

Those flowers have been conjured.

William strode on ahead with his long coat flapping and the hem catching on the thorny flower stalks. He paused for a moment to pull it free, bent down and picked a flower. 'For you.' He reached out to hand Vreni the bloom.

The petals quivered, she was sure of it. Yes, there it was again, the slightest movement rippling across the flower. Then the petals appeared to come loose from the stalk, flapped gently and stretched, ruffling and unfolding, and the flower was transformed into an oddly proportioned butterfly.

Each of the butterfly's petal-wings was larger than Vreni's outstretched hand, but its body was tiny, almost hidden between the oversized wings. There was movement all around them. Twenty or more flowers were opening and transforming. When each was fully open it rested on the thorny stalks, the wings rising and falling in unison, with a rhythm reminiscent of breathing. Every butterfly had one large eye on each of its wings. Some pairs were blue, others green or brown.

'It blinked.' William stared at the butterfly creature on top of the stalk he still held in his hand.

Vreni watched the eyes on the wings blink once, then again. 'This can't be a good thing,' she said, as the eyes on each wing of every one of the woken creatures blinked in unison.

William's butterfly blinked again and ruffled its wings. Then it flapped gently into the air and hovered level with his face. The others followed and soon the small rabble of creatures was flapping and hovering around him. The leader was watching, looking at William and Vreni in turn. It landed lightly on William's head. Vreni was captivated. They seemed to be lingering in the air so peacefully.

Another blink and everything changed.

In a swift blur of wings, the creature had wrapped itself around William's head, covering his face. At least five of the creatures followed the first, moving with blinding speed, wrapping themselves, layer upon layer, over William's face.

Vreni heard his stifled screams, and watched as he clawed at the wings that gripped his face. He thrashed and contorted in his effort to pry them loose. Then his cries faded and he sank to his knees, collapsing onto the ground.

Vreni stood frozen for a disbelieving moment, trying to make sense of what she was seeing. Then she reached out, prying at the wings that seemed glued to William's face.

Your knife, Vreni, Anna said.

As Vreni pulled the knife from its pouch, she felt the first feather-soft wing brush her own face. She grabbed for it and pulled the creature from her skin. Slicing madly at it with her knife, she separated the body from the wings, and the creature shrivelled and turned brown. She reached for another that had landed on her head and then stabbed at the others waiting in the air. She sliced again and again. Each severed corpse withered where it fell.

She lunged for William. He had stopped fighting now and his legs shuddered weakly. She pried her fingers under the top butterfly, severing its wings from its body.

'Get *off* him,' she yelled, tears blurring her vision.

He still lives, Anna said. *You're doing well. Keep going.*

Vreni clawed each creature loose and cut away its body, stopping only to slash at those that flew towards them for a fresh attack. Time seemed to drag. She urged her fingers to move more quickly through the layers that *entombed* William's head. Finally she cut through the last set of wings, watching them desiccate against William's pale skin. He gasped a ragged howling breath, then coughed and sobbed.

'You're safe, they're dead,' Vreni said, pulling him close as she fended off the last of the circling creatures. She realised how desperately she needed to hold him after watching him struggling on the ground.

Anna's voice came urgently in her ear: *Smother-flies: old magic and strong. Smother-flies are drawn to the rhythm of the breath. You'll wake more of them if you can't quiet*

William's breathing. Try to hold your breath as you walk through them and they won't be able to sense you.

William needed time they didn't have, but Vreni let him rest a moment longer. She hummed quietly to disguise the rhythm of his breathing, and added a soothing charm to the quiet tune.

When he was still she quickly told him what Anna had said. 'We have to go now.' She loosened her arms from around him, and then stood and reached out her hand.

William's hand was cold and damp in hers. His eyes still shone with fear as they walked through the field of sleeping smother-flies. Vreni held her breath until it burned and she was lightheaded, then stifled a shallow half-breath.

At the edge of the field of flowers they stood for a moment, staring back at the deadly blooms, not willing to chance filling their hungry lungs. When Vreni finally allowed herself to take a deep breath, it was sweet and energising—and painful.

William walked on beside her, silent except for the sound of his breathing, which was deep and long, like he was feasting on the air.

'Air,' she said. 'The *absence* of air as a defence.' She shuddered.

'Only fire left,' he coughed, squeezing her hand tightly.

'Only,' she said quietly.

—∿—

They were close to the building now, but the densely planted grove of birch trees that encircled it hid them from the eyes of any guard. They tried to check their position so that when they came out on the other side of this ring of forest they wouldn't be too close to the main entrance and the guard.

It was shady and cool as they stepped under the trees. The sunlight and shadows made dappled patterns on the leaves that blanketed the ground.

'Trees and fire,' William said. 'It's a bit of a no-brainer, I suppose.'

This last defence shouldn't offer much of a challenge, Anna said. *At least I hope not. They would be expecting most people to be dead before they got this far.*

'Anna said this last defence might be small. Just one extra precaution,' Vreni said, crossing her fingers.

As they walked on, a light shower of orange and red leaves fell from the thick canopy above, touching them gently before landing with the others that thickly covered the ground. The rust-coloured carpet of leaves crunched quietly with each step.

As they reached what they judged to be the halfway point through the small forest, the fall of leaves increased, although they still fluttered down slowly. Then the leaves that landed on their shoulders began to burst into flames.

'This is it. Still got your fingers crossed?' William brushed a burning leaf from Vreni's shoulder.

They walked on underneath the trees. The rain of leaves grew heavier. Now it was ten leaves, more, burning on their clothes, in their hair. They swept them off each other but the shower of fiery leaves was increasing. Now the burning leaves were reaching the ground and setting fire to the ones that already lay there. William took off his coat and pulled Vreni under it, shielding them from the leaves that ignited as soon as they touched down on a surface.

'We need to get out of here,' William said. 'Soon the fire on the ground will be a huge problem.'

The leaves on the ground feel your footfalls, Anna explained. *They tell the other leaves to drop from the trees. Whether you move fast or slow, the leaves will know you're there.*

William watched Vreni, knowing she was listening to Anna's voice. 'Any advice?'

'Run,' Vreni said.

They huddled close under the heavy coat and ran towards the tree line, leaping over patches of burning leaves as they went. The air around them was thick with acrid grey-blue smoke that couldn't escape through the thick canopy.

They burst out of the trees. Their eyes burned and they could hardly see. Throats scorched and breathless, they ran across the innermost circle of lawn and threw themselves onto the ground close to the wall. They were a long way around the southern curve of the building, far from where the guard was likely to be, but they waited, trying to stifle the sound of their coughing.

Labyrinth

The flames had smouldered low and quickly burned out, and the smoke seeped away into the leafy treetops. Vreni and William clung to each other and waited, hearts racing. Nothing. They dared a cough. Nothing. It seemed, for now, that they hadn't been detected.

'So those were the AlGuild pets.' William looked back over the grounds towards the south. 'What next?'

'Haven't you had enough?'

'No, but why didn't you use the charms?'

'Anna said not to use them yet,' she answered. 'She said that using magic out here would draw attention to us.'

'After that back there, I suppose anyone who was watching would believe we were dead.'

'And we still have the charms to use once we're inside,' Vreni said, as much to reassure herself as William.

'Those charms, will they really work? The Wise Sisters don't seem to do much abracadabra sort of magic. Will we have what we need to keep ourselves alive in there?'

'While I've been at Mežs Mājas I've learned that the magic works because of the contributions made by so many of the Sisters. The old magic is more about the intentions of the Sisters than abracadabra.' She smiled. 'It's about unity. So many of them—of us—have made sacrifices. Mine is to walk the labyrinth and use my power to release the stored magic of their spells. I have to believe that all these sacrifices will be rewarded and the charms will work.'

Rest a while, Anna interrupted. *Eat. Drink. If William still has the bundle Emma gave him, open it now.*

'Anna says you have a bundle that contains food and drink,' Vreni said.

'What, this?' William pulled a small cloth-bound bundle from the inside pocket of his coat. 'I hope you're not too hungry.'

'The sisters are very good at storage.' She laughed, thinking of the tiny whisper-birds.

She pulled at the wax seal that held the parcel closed and felt a tingling in her hands as she pried away the thick wax. A tiny ball of energy sparked where the seal had been broken, fizzing and flowing, trickling inside the wrapping.

She laid the parcel on the grass and pulled open the cloth. The contents inside gave the slightest quiver before expanding and taking form, growing just as the whisper-birds had done. When the transformation was complete, the bundle contained a simple meal of cheese and blackbread, a mound of juicy red berries and a bottle of water.

William stared disbelievingly.

Vreni took one of the berries and held it gently between her fingers. She looked closely at the perfect red spheres clustered together. 'I love summer berries. They taste so good. The only berries that taste better than these are the ones you find for yourself.'

She offered a berry to William and took another for herself, eating it slowly.

'When I was little, in the summertime back in Vārve,' she said, 'we used to go looking for wild berries and mushrooms in the forest. We would pack a lunch, and take baskets and buckets and the dogs. We'd walk for hours in the dappled shade. It was always so cool inside the forest.' She smiled. Her eyes were looking back through time. 'Our tutor, a long time before Sabina, of course, showed Rita and me a secret way of finding the best, juiciest berries.'

'How?' he asked, handing her some cheese and bread.

'We used to ask the birds,' she replied. 'Well, we didn't *ask* them, we eavesdropped on them. We learned how to walk quietly under the trees and listen. It's easy once you know what the birds are saying.'

'You talked to the birds?'

'No. We listened. When a mother bird found a stalk heavy with ripe fruit she would sing and sing. She was saying three things when she sang.'

'What did she say?'

'First the mother bird would be saying thank you for the berries, because today her babies would not be hungry. Second, she would be bragging and celebrating being so good at finding berries. And third, she would be calling to all the other mother birds to share her luck with them. All the birds share like that, because they know that it's the nature of good times and bad times to come whenever they please. The birds know that a challenge is made easier by sharing it. That's how the Wise Sisters do it, too. They work together to achieve far greater things than any one of them could accomplish alone.'

Thank you, Vreni, Anna said quietly.

'Do you miss Vārve?' William asked.

Vreni gave a tiny nod. 'But I think that at Mežs Mājas I have something that feels the same. No, better. Home is a different thing now than what I thought it was.'

'We could go there one day, if you like, to Vārve. You could show me how to search for berries and mushrooms. One day, when we're both free to make our own plans.'

'Why are you doing this?' Vreni asked quietly. 'This is not your fight.'

William stared at the ground for a long moment before he spoke. 'Two reasons, I think. First, because I'm selfish—'

'In what way are you selfish? Look at all you've done for Rita and me already.'

'Well, yeah, but I want to be here for *me*.' He smiled at her. 'I've met this girl who can do magic and seems to live forever, and then she invites me on the adventure of my lifetime so far.'

He stopped and looked back at the ground and then continued, more serious now. 'You're not the only one who's been controlled by your family, Vreni. I've done what I've been told all my life. I was sent to a boarding school with high walls when I was young, and now my new walls are my father's expectations—study, and follow in his footsteps. So this is about me finally getting to do something that hasn't been planned for me.'

'You've got the dancing,' Vreni said, trying to lighten the mood.

He smiled. 'I wonder what my father would say if he knew about the dance parties.'

'And what's the second reason?'

'Well, that seems less clear, but a feeling that I wouldn't be anywhere else but here, and that I need to go wherever you're going.' He rubbed his hands together and smiled. 'I don't know, maybe you've put a spell on me.'

'You've caught me out, but it was only a spell to make you dance with me.' Vreni laughed to cover the slick of dread that was flowing through her mind. Could the Sisters make William be here against his will, by magic? She had to believe they hadn't done that. After all, she'd been told that the magic would only work if the sacrifice were given willingly.

They finished their meal in silence.

Looking out from where they sat, there was no sign of their passage from the fence to the building. The lawns and gardens of the compound seemed ordered and peaceful. The scene was the public image of AIGuild. It was scenes like this that appeared on the corporate website for AIGuild research and development, with lots of glossy photos and some very vague corporate information. Anything useful like projects, or current staff and management, were only available with a password.

From the fence, the building blended into the low hills that surrounded it, but up close it loomed over them like a smooth, circular monolith. It was as wide as a football field, with a roof perhaps ten metres high. The outer surface of the building was dotted with evenly spaced windows, which sat high on the walls to allow in the light but were too high for anyone to see in.

Or out, Vreni hoped. She felt relieved to know they probably hadn't been seen.

The large rectangular window panes mirrored the now peaceful gardens. The shining patches of glass continued around the curve of the building. None showed any evidence that they could be opened.

They stayed close to the wall as they moved towards the east side of the building, edging closer to the entrance. A pathway, elaborately paved with the AIGuild logo, linked the entrance to the front gate and the still deserted carpark.

'You can't fault them on corporate image,' William joked.

'Well, not unless you take a walk through their Pleasure Gardens.'

After a few more silent steps, the front entrance came into view around the curve of the building.

'There's the keypad, but what can we do about the guard?' William whispered.

'I'll call him off.' Vreni remembered the guard in the dream realm, and hoped her skill with voice would work again. 'We won't have long.'

She took a calming breath and watched the guard for a long moment, preparing to send her false message around the far side of the building.

'Hey, Harry, I thought these windows were toughened glass. This looks like a crack,' said the false voice.

'What?' The guard looked surprised. He hurried away from the door towards the unexpected voice.

'You knew his name was Harry? You do have some skills,' William said.

'Yeah, reading skills. He had a name tag.'

She pulled William toward the polished glass door and the bio-lock pad. He held his key amulet in one hand and placed the other, palm down, on the sensor pad. The door clicked and released a hiss of air. They opened the door just wide enough to slide inside and hid themselves in a shallow alcove at the side of the doorway.

Vreni watched the door, which was still slightly ajar. It hissed as it closed maddeningly slowly and then finally clicked.

Through the window they saw the guard return to his post outside the door, looking confused. Vreni remembered the fate of the young guard she used her voice on in the palace and shuddered, hoping Harry wouldn't meet a similar fate because of her.

The foyer of the building looked just as corporate as the entryway outside. It was furnished with sleek leather sofas and low glass tables. One white wall contained an oversized painting in a weighty gold frame, and the other was adorned with the AIGuild logo and its vague mission statement. The reception desk was unattended and there was a layer of dust on it, and also on the coffee machine that sat unused in the corner.

'This looks like it's all for show,' William said.

She nodded. 'They just need it to look normal from the door.'

She pointed past the dusty, overgrown potted palms to where the glaring white facade ended suddenly, not far inside the corridor that led into the rest of the building. She chanced a quick look through the glass door to make sure they remained undiscovered, then grabbed William's arm and they moved quickly into the passageway out of sight.

Hoard

The corridor leading out of the foyer changed abruptly from smooth white plaster to rough damp stone. It reminded Vreni of the walls in her grandmother's palace. She stood listening, straining her ears for any sign that they weren't alone, but the space inside the passageway was filled with a thick silence; it was so quiet she could hear her hand moving over the rough stonework wall.

'That was definitely all for show,' she said, pointing back to the foyer.

She inhaled, curious; the air smelled moist like earth and bark after rain, but lingering on the still air was the scent of something else. The faint odour made her think of burnt spice or strong vinegar, something sour and acrid.

She looked as far as she could along the corridor. She held her breath, expecting someone or something to appear and stop them. After the Pleasure Gardens, she could only imagine what might be done to stop them in here.

She nudged William. 'Let's go.'

They set off cautiously, still expecting to have been discovered and confronted at any moment. The narrow passageway ran straight for a short distance, then turned to the left and curved in a clockwise direction. The roof was much lower here than it had been in the foyer. They had moved away from the light at the entrance, but it wasn't any darker. There was light, but no light source was evident; it was just light.

Because of the curve of the passageway, they could only see a few metres ahead. They soon lost any idea of the distance they had come. It was silent within the labyrinth, and even the words they dared utter seemed to soak into the walls as they spoke them. The passageway remained unchanged, continuing to sweep clockwise.

'Candles,' Vreni muttered.

'Where?' William's voice was urgent.

'Not here, in the dream realm. The hallways of the palace had small alcoves in the walls every few metres holding candles. If we had those here we could judge how far we'd come.'

'I'd rather know how far we have to go.'

There was nothing to do but continue. The cobbled floor consumed the sound of their footfalls as they walked.

—◊◊◊—

The curve of the passageway began to straighten out. Suddenly Vreni was alert again. She threw her arm across William's chest defensively.

'Stop,' she whispered.

'What?' William looked up with wide eyes.

'Something's new, slow down,' she said, scanning the path ahead, watchful for threats.

It's a turning point, Anna said. *Try to remember the drawings of the labyrinth we showed you.*

Vreni moved cautiously up to the end of the wall. The passageway turned back on itself. The turning point was decorated with vines, leaves and budding flowers that had been carved into the stonework. The designs twisted their way up into a shallow, domed roof that rose from the passageway they were standing in and then dropped down again as the corridor switched back on itself and departed the turning space.

Vreni turned slowly. Her eyes followed the trailing vines across the dome. She finished her circling turn and found herself face to face with a creature staring down at her from the high ledge of an alcove at the end of the wall. She jumped back, gulping down a sourness that rose in her throat, and reached for her knife.

William rushed to her side. Following her gaze, he also jumped at the sight of the peering stone face.

It's a grotesque, Anna said, *a stone creature.*

'Carved in stone,' Vreni said, laughing at their over reaction.

It was more likely turned into stone. The alchemists would rather conjure and entrap a thing than create a thing.

'Its eyes seem to follow you around the room,' William said.

Vreni looked at the grotesque and shivered. Light glinted from its polished stone eyes.

They turned away from the staring goblin and entered the stone passage at the other side of the turning. Now the path swept in an anticlockwise direction, with the same seamlessness as before.

Vreni thought back to the diagram of the labyrinth in the *Book of Wisdoms*. She tried to draw what she remembered in her mind, adding in the details she was discovering. Those details could be useful later. Perhaps what she was seeing would be more meaningful to Sabina and Anna than it was to her at the moment.

William was walking ahead of her, counting steps. Their eyes met for a moment, but he turned forward again and continued counting silently to himself.

The anticlockwise path was longer than the first clockwise curve. The labyrinth was a set of concentric circles that folded back on themselves. First it would take them deep into the building, and then back out to its edge before they would finally turn inwards again, to reach the very centre where the alchemists would be hiding their most precious possessions. That was where the remaining sleeping potion should be. Vreni wondered what else they would find there.

William nudged her. He pointed up ahead. The light was brighter there, and the passageway straightened again, but this time it also widened slightly. They flattened themselves against the wall and listened.

They heard a snuffle, then a mumbled growl. The noise sounded like words being spoken. They strained to hear if they were real words, and if so, who, or what, was speaking.

'... seven, eight, nine, ten, eleven ...' There was a metallic rattle then a shuffling noise. The voice faded and returned again. '... twenty-two, twenty-three, twenty-four, more of those is nice, yes, Hoard needs more of those.' There was a loud snorting, sniffing sound, then the voice was weeping. 'Yes, food is nice, too. Hoard is so hungry.' The voice sobbed for a while and then quietened, but the sniffing remained.

They stood pressed into the last curve of the wall. William caught her eye and then reached down and touched her necklace, his eyes asking if she really could use the magic they had been promised was contained in the charms.

She was glad she couldn't answer. She trusted the magic in the charms, but she had less trust in her own ability to call the magic into being. She leaned towards William and kissed him. He pulled away from her abruptly.

It took her a moment to realise that he hadn't pulled away; he had been snatched away. She stifled a scream when she saw a large creature silhouetted in the bright light dragging William into the circular space ahead.

It hasn't seen you, Vreni, Anna said urgently. *Stay hidden.*

Vreni pressed herself hard against the wall. She held her teeth tightly together to stop herself from crying out, and strained her eyes to the side to get a better look at what had taken William.

William had been lifted off the ground and dragged away as though he was a doll. Now he was thrashing and kicking into the creature's filth-encrusted lower limbs, trying to free himself. The creature didn't look right to Vreni. It appeared to have four arms, or four legs, or maybe more. *Maybe there's more than one of them.*

Vreni stayed nailed to the wall, feeling the rough stone pressing sharply into her back. She dared to turn her head and stare as the monster shambled back into the light. She heard a metallic rattling. Then she thought she could hear humming and quiet laughing.

She prised herself from the wall and moved forward slowly. At the edge of the circle of light, she came to a large pile of rags and tattered cushions. The sharp stink of urine and some unimaginable filth jabbed at her nostrils. She gagged as she crept up close to the pile and pulled the rags around her, creating a hiding place.

As she scanned the area more carefully, she realised she was at another turning point in the passage. It had been made wider here to make room for this thing, whatever it was.

On the other side of the circle, William struggled against the gruesome shambles of arms and legs. The creature stood on several mismatched legs, but there were some other, stray limbs dangling down from the lower part of its bloated body.

Vreni could see now that it was only one creature, but it had four arms protruding from its front, which were now tying William to a metal loop that hung from the far wall, and more arms sticking out the back of its body. Many of the arms were withered and twisted, and the skin of each was different—pale, dark, smooth, hairy.

Vreni tried to count the arms as the creature loped about awkwardly. The fleshy collection of half-dead arms was crowded at odd angles all around the lumpy body. She finally counted eight mismatched legs, three of them flopping, too misshapen to reach the floor, but she couldn't count all the arms on the patchwork abomination. Its skin was crisscrossed with puckered lines where the pieces had somehow been fused together.

William continued to struggle, but the creature had tied his hands to the wall above his head. He was stretched out, his feet barely touching the floor.

The monster huffed at him and shuffled to the centre of the floor. It was dragging a heavy chain. The chain, which was manacled to the ankle of one of its thick legs, stretched out across the floor and was firmly attached to a steel ring on the wall above the stinking pile of rags where Vreni was hiding. She realised this must be its bed, and this bend in the passageway was its home and all the life the creature knew.

The wretched thing began to hum again, and then it started singing. 'You heard me crying!' The creature tilted its head and sang out towards something or someone who wasn't there. 'Hoard was so hungry, food is so nice. Hoard wanted to be more, more of Hoard is so nice. Now Hoard can collect more pieces and not be so lonely.'

Vreni watched, horrified and amazed. As the creature sang she could see its faces. Just like its arms and legs, the hoard had many faces, or parts of faces. Its mouths sang out. The tuneless music came from one of the mouths, which was surrounded by the pudgy folds of its face, but as it sang the ghastly song, the lips of other mouths, dotted here and there around its head, neck and shoulders, moved in unison in an attempt to join in the grisly chant.

For every mouth that adorned the bloated, pale body there were pairs of eyes and ears in measure. Not arranged in sets that became simply a misplaced face, but a collection of misshapen and mutilated ears were scattered around the head and shoulders, and as many shrivelled, suppurating eyes, some milky and dead, some staring off in all directions.

And there was a tail. On the monster's back, a dog's tail wagged.

The creature kept singing. 'Hoard is thankful, Hoard has food, food is so nice, and more parts for Hoard, and more parts makes Hoard happy. Thank you, master.'

William finally cast his eyes towards her hiding place and she risked a wave. He responded with a minute half-smile.

To have created a hoard, how heartless, Anna said. A hoard's hunger for food is insatiable. The only thing greater is its hunger to belong, to be near others. It's the loneliest of all creatures, so it collects pieces of its victims to form a crowd around itself, in the hope that it won't feel so lonely.

Before this happened to this hoard it would have been a good man. The alchemists captured him and emptied out his heart. Now the hoard needs to devour flesh to stay alive. It then knits the remnants of its victims into itself to ease the aching loneliness that torments its heart.

Vreni lifted the charms that were strung around her neck, hoping that Sabina would see her question: *what charms would she use?*

Sabina had seen, and Anna replied: *The hoard will be fascinated by the sound of a voice, but being trapped in here means it lives with silence most of the time. You have the singing and the chants of the Sisters to fill the air with sound, and you need something to catch its eye, to distract it.*

Anna's voice ceased. Vreni wanted to be told more. It was all so cryptic.

She steadied her breathing and stared at the charms. The final choices and the speaking of intention was her contribution to the spell. She knew she must decide for herself and will it into being. The songs of the Sisters swirled inside the glass capsule. Then Vreni remembered the swarm of bumblebees that sat frozen inside another charm.

She signalled William to talk to the hoard.

The hoard leaned in close to William and sniffed at him. All the noses joined in the sniffing. Next it licked the side of his face. The other mouths made feeble sucking noises. All William could do was hold his breath against the stench of the beast's drooling mouth and step as far to the right as his bonds would allow him.

He coughed and started to speak. 'Hello, I'm William,' he choked.

The creature drew back and smiled at him. 'You talk to Hoard. Talk is so nice.' The hoard leaned closer again for another noisy sniff, and licked its very wet lips.

'So your name is Hoard. Do you have another name?

'Once I did, a name that was so nice, but the silence took it and the others that are Hoard mumbled lots of names.' It danced around as if to show off its gruesome collection. 'Their names got in the way. But we are all Hoard now.'

'How long have you lived here?' William said, trying to hold the hoard's attention.

'Long, so long, and so alone, and so very hungry.' The hoard came closer again and bought its foul mouth up to William's face. Its lips and tongue lightly touched its lips captive's skin to taste him once more.

William shuddered violently.

The creature continued to lean over him. There was a rasping noise as it sharpened its yellow nails against the stone wall. 'So hungry.'

It inspected the razor sharp claws that curled from each fingertip before pushing a bony knuckle into the flesh on William's belly.

'Hoard has food, food is so nice,' it said, and licked its lips. 'Hoard can be more, more is so nice.' It ran its sharpened claws lightly over William's arms and face, as if trying to decide which parts of him to add to its collection. 'Hoard has food, food is so nice, Hoard can be more ...'

The hoard seemed to be dancing with excitement. It gripped William's arms and shook him.

Vreni knew she had to act now. The hoard's chain wasn't very long. If she could free William they could run and get out of its reach. She took three charms from her necklace.

The hoard continued its strangled singing, which would cover the sound of her voice. The charms full of swirling music would be first. She held them in her palm. She found the words somewhere within her and let them spill over the shining sphere.

'Canon and cadence, sweet voices singing out,
The melodies will fill the air until they are a shout.
Sing my sisters, sing with all your heart.'

The skin of the tiny orbs split and peeled away as Vreni's words moved across it. Through the mist that spread across her hand, she heard a quiet chant. The voices grew louder as the mist lifted into the air and drifted towards the hoard.

It looked around, its eyes darting in all directions. 'Who's there? Stop singing!' it growled. The freed voices filled the circle that was the hoard's world. 'Enough! Hoard is singing.'

Its arms swung heavily as it twisted and turned. It tripped over its bulky chain as it looked for the source of the sound. The voices swam around it. The chanting was now accompanied by singing. The hoard moaned from all of its many mouths.

Vreni reached for her second weapon, a swarm of tiny bumblebees that had been held in mid-flight inside another of the small glass spheres. She rolled the bauble gently between her palms to warm the bees and wake them.

'Awake now and take to the wing,
Fly and buzz, swarm and sting.
Distracting, enraging and saddening,
Tormenting and maddening.'

The glass of the charm dissolved in Vreni's palm. The bees began circling in a miniature hive dance. Like the whisper-birds, they doubled and redoubled in size as they danced around on her palm. They lifted from her hand and swept around the room, spiralling up towards the hoard. The singing and chanting was growing to a crescendo.

The hoard reached feebly with its malformed collection of hands, trying to cover its numerous ears. 'No more singing,' it pleaded to the unseen voices. 'Silence is so nice.' It twisted and staggered around. 'No more singing.'

The bees swept past the hoard. It wailed, swatting at them as they swarmed around its head. It yelped as the bees started to sting. It was slapping wildly at itself, trying to fight off the fast-moving attackers. Its arms and legs took on the fight without waiting for the hoard's direction. It stumbled and faltered, tripping again and again on its heavy chain.

The air was filled with the rhythmic chanting and harmonies of the Sisters, the unceasing drone of the swarming bees, and the frantic bawling of the hoard as it continued to fight its unseen menace.

Vreni knew the hoard's chain only allowed it to reach a short way into either passageway. As long as it couldn't pull hard enough to wrench the chain free from the wall, they could be outside of its reach soon enough. She took her chance and ran from the pile of rags towards William.

The hoard's arms continued to beat the air, trying to swat the bees. She ducked under its flailing hands, the needle-sharp claws just missing her face. As it turned, one of its stunted legs swung freely and struck Vreni in the ribs. She staggered, landing hard on the floor. Her knee burned and her eyes stung with tears. She pulled herself up from the floor and limped to William.

She looked up. No! She couldn't reach William's hands tied high on the wall. Trying to block out the hoard's distracted yelping, she took a step back and threw herself at William.

He groaned.

'Sorry,' she whispered.

Finding a small foothold in the stone wall, she clambered up his body and rested her knee on his shoulder. She pulled out her knife and cut through the frayed rags that bound his wrists to the iron ring. He lowered his hands, she lost her balance and they crashed to the floor. He bent quickly and pulled her to her feet.

The hoard spun around and saw that William was free. 'No!' it roared. 'Hoard's food! Hoard's more!'

Vreni pulled William towards the narrowing passageway on the far side of the stone circle that was the hoard's prison. Just a few metres and they would be out of its vile reach. They ran, stumbling as they clung to each other. The hoard's demands dissolved into angry bellows of frustration. Its feet made heavy, arrhythmic thudding sounds on the stone floor behind them.

Vreni felt William suddenly slow down behind her and looked over her shoulder. The hoard was pulling on William's flapping coat with one crooked arm. Then she saw a second arm, with its hand filled with razor-like claws, sweep across William's face. The claws caught on his cheek.

William screamed and dipped his head, trying to avoid the worst of the gouging attack.

Vreni pulled William's arm with all the strength she had left.

The hoard caught a foot in its chain and tripped, toppling into the wall and smacking its gruesome head against the stone. It staggered as it tried to get to its feet. Vreni used the moment to haul William into the narrowing passageway that had turned back on itself and was sweeping clockwise again.

The hoard was howling in defeat behind them, its calls growing more distant with every step. Vreni couldn't bring herself to stop. They ran on for some distance until William misjudged the curve of the wall and hit it heavily.

'Stop, Vreni, we're safe here,' he panted.

'But—' She turned and froze.

William's face was slashed. Three deep gashes oozed blood that dripped down his left cheek onto his neck and soaked his collar. A fourth cut above his right eye had somehow, luckily, glanced over the eye itself before scraping across his right cheek. He staggered and slid down the rough wall. He sat shaking violently.

Vreni sat beside him and took a closer look at his face. He winced at her touch, but remained silent. She retrieved from his coat pocket the cloth that their lunch had been wrapped in and laid it across his wounded cheek.

'I wish I could do more.' She squeezed his hand.

He smiled weakly. Placing his hand on the makeshift bandage on his face, he stood up. 'Let's get going,' he said quietly.

She took a breath to speak but then changed her mind. He grabbed her hand and they continued along the curving passageway.

Temptation

*Our deepest desires are treasures. We hide
them inside ourselves, where we believe them
to be safe. These desires can be our greatest
strengths, or our most vexing weaknesses.*
~ Pratigs Māsa, *Book of Wisdoms*

The arc of the cobbled passageway swept on. Each stone
in the wall melted into the next, and the ones behind
them fell away into nothing as the curve devoured them.
They trudged on, each step heavy with effort. They walked
together but were somehow separate.

Vreni knew from the map she had contrived with
her mind's eye that this ring of the labyrinth would be
slightly longer again than the one that had led them to
their encounter with the hoard, but knowing it would be
a greater distance to the next turn didn't ease the dread
she felt about what they would meet there.

She wanted to talk to William, to discuss strategy and
calm her fears about what they might face next.

She glanced at him out of the corner of her eye. He was
stooped over, his head bowed, clutching his face tenderly.

She decided he deserved the consolation of the little time they might have to be alone with his pain and to settle his thoughts. *I can't burden him with my fears now.*

Vreni knew Sabina would be listening, but if she asked questions or spoke her fears out loud so the Sisters could hear her and offer advice or words of reassurance, William would hear her too. He would hear her fear and her crumbling confidence. She didn't want to force him to withdraw from his fallow, thought-filled state just to help her feel better.

She watched him, but left him to his thoughts for a little longer. He was the injured one, while she was only scared. She had chosen to do this thing rather than wait for someone else to do it for her, so she must do it, even if it was frightening. She hung her head and concentrated on their feet shuffling slowly on.

The mysterious soft glow of the passageway was growing stronger. In front of them the curve was straightening and the space glowed more brightly. Vreni couldn't leave William to his thoughts any longer. She slid her hand into his and squeezed.

His shuffling steps stopped and he looked up, wincing as he straightened. 'What next?' His voice wavered.

'Stay here. I'll go and look.'

Vreni let go of William's hand and nudged his shoulders firmly against the wall to reinforce the idea that he should stay there, and, she hoped, to make herself look more confident than she felt. She walked slowly but purposefully towards the brightening light, not trusting herself to look him in the eye in case she faltered.

The warmly lit space ahead was about the same size as the last turning point. She heard water flowing somewhere. She could smell the freshness of it. Her throat suddenly ached, feeling incredibly dry. Her mouth tasted brackish. All she could think of was drinking cool, clean water.

She flattened herself against the last curve of the wall and dared to look out into the space. It was deserted. There was no one and nothing to be seen. Her attention was drawn again to the sound of running water; a small spigot was trickling water into a stone basin carved into the far wall. In the centre of the circular space was a collection of low leather sofas and velvet stools strewn with silk cushions, surrounding a large, highly polished wooden chest that was inlaid with brass.

Vreni's legs suddenly felt limp and she found it hard to lift her feet. The music of the flowing water filled her awareness.

She turned to signal for William to join her, but he was leaning against the wall with his eyes closed. She quickly walked back to him, feeling happy that she could offer the hope of some comfort and a place to rest, even if they could only stay for a while.

'William,' she whispered, rubbing his rounded shoulders. 'So far I can't see any trouble up ahead, but there was no danger at the first turn, so we might be lucky.'

She led him, quiet and stooped, to the circular space of the third turning point. She heard him inhale deeply and knew that he had smelled the water. His uninjured eye opened more fully and took in the scene.

'I'm so thirsty.' He flopped down onto a sofa, sagging against one of the oversized cushions. He patted his pocket and reached into it, retrieving the water bottle he had kept from their lunch bundle. It had miraculously survived without breaking during their encounter with the hoard.

'You first.' William handed Vreni the bottle.

She wanted to argue but her tongue was burning, sticky and sour.

The water trickled from the spigot maddeningly slowly. She filled the bottle three times and drank each thirstily before she began to feel the dry bitterness in her throat washing away. She filled the bottle for William and took it back to where he rested among the cushions.

She trailed backward and forward between the spigot and the sofa, bringing him water, continually scanning the space as she did so, alert for danger.

This turning point was about the same size as the one that had served as the hoard's prison. The space was decorated similarly to the first, except with much more elaborate detail. There were pools of indigo shadow around the room, but where there was light, intricate designs and details were carved into the walls. There were vines and flowers, but instead of the staring face of a grotesque, there were birds.

On the bottom half of the walls were geometric designs creating borders that framed scenes of gardens and landscapes. From these frames, the carved vines twisted and curved up the smooth stone walls towards the domed ceiling.

Vreni's eyes followed the creeping vines upward and saw that the ceiling of the chamber held a sea of gemstone stars. She thought for a moment of the dream room back at Mežs Mājas and could almost hear the Sisters' voices singing. She allowed herself to float away, surrounded by the warm sea of imagined sound, and some of the tension slipped from her shoulders.

'Nice,' William said quietly.

'What?' she asked absent mindedly.

'The tune, very nice.'

'Thanks, I was just daydreaming, I must've started humming out loud.' She felt a little self-conscious and confused because she couldn't remember starting to hum, even quietly.

'Come and rest,' he urged.

Suddenly Vreni felt exhausted. She filled the bottle once more and drank slowly. 'I need to clean your wounds.'

She removed her scarf and wet one end in the stone basin, then returned to the sofa and finally sat. It felt like paradise. The coolness of the leather against her arms was soothing and mounds of velvet cushions surrounded her, cradling her tried muscles. She breathed deeply, feeling her body go limp at last. She would have been happy to curl into the generous softness of it all and turn her back on everything. She sighed deeply and closed her eyes for just a moment.

William fidgeted restlessly next to her. She reluctantly lifted her head from the cushions and shook it gently to focus her thoughts. She leaned towards him and timidly pulled away the cloth that had been covering his wounds.

Gently, she cleaned the filth and dried blood away from the cuts. She was relieved to see that the cut that ran across his right eye was mercifully slight. His sight would be safe, but the gashes in his left cheek were deep and angry looking. They had stopped bleeding, but they were now oozing a yellow watery mess that didn't look like stopping any time soon.

'So am I still your handsome prince?' he joked quietly.

'Indeed, sir,' she said. 'We princesses like our heroes to look rugged and adventure-worn. Now keep still, brave prince, so I can sooth your wounds.'

She cleaned the gashes as well as she could, and then bandaged them using the only thing available, her scarf. She wrapped the scarf around his forehead, covering the cut above his eyes, and then circled it around once more, this time below his eyes and across his nose, binding the deep gouges in an effort to pull the ragged edges together and soak up the liquid that oozed profusely from them. The makeshift bandage covered most of William's face.

Now that the wounds were covered, she looked at him and smiled. He looked like a bank robber or a masked hero from an old black-and-white movie. She tied the two ends of the scarf together to secure the bandage and kissed him gently on the lips. His eyes sparkled through the swelling.

Vreni rested her head against the soft cushions again. She felt the hardness inside her stomach softening a little. Her thoughts drifted to the first time she had kissed William on the darkened dance floor, surrounded by music and flashing colour.

'Yes!' William exclaimed joyfully. 'I am so hungry,'

She opened her eyes. William had lifted the lid of the wooden chest and was picking through the boxes and bundles inside. He opened a few of them.

He laughed. 'Bananas, nuts, bread that's not black.'

'There's nothing wrong with blackbread,' Vreni scoffed. 'Mmm, blackbread and liverwurst.'

'Delicious, I'm sure.' He pulled a face and reached for a crusty bread roll.

'Should we take a chance on eating any of it, considering where we are?' she asked warily.

'I'll take it slowly.' He pulled a small piece of bread off the corner of the roll and put it in his mouth without chewing. 'I know it's not much of a precaution, but feeling for a mouth reaction can help identify dangerous plants and things in the bush, so maybe it'll help here. So far it feels okay.' he said, talking around the bread.

'Maybe there'll be some apple bread in there, or cheesecake, something sweet,' Vreni said wistfully.

'Turkish delight,' William added.

'My prince, you are indeed exotic.'

'*Your* prince?' His eyes sparkled again from within the bandages.

Vreni shoved her shoulder into his. 'Seeing as you're not poisoned yet, let's try something else—slowly.'

They lifted the boxes and bundles out of the chest and closed the lid, using it as a table. Inside the parcels they found berries and cheese, small savoury pies, a pot of smooth liverwurst and a loaf of heavy blackbread.

They opened the lid of a round silver tin and a delicious sweet smell rose up, dancing on their nostrils. The tin contained a dazzling array of sweets: tiny bite-size portions, each nestled in colourful paper wrappers. There were fruit jellies, fine biscuits, cubes of Turkish delight studded with pistachio nuts, even tiny round cheesecakes and chocolate truffles.

A glass bottle held a deep plum-coloured liquid, which stirred with tiny bubbles when the lid was opened. It smelled of berries and cinnamon, and tasted sweet and refreshing.

At first they explored the picnic with caution, nibbling tiny pieces of foods and waiting for any sign of danger, but with each morsel they sampled their cares diminished. They paid attention only to their hunger, and ate.

Vreni looked across the remnants of food sitting on the lid of the chest. She was surprised she had eaten so much without remembering having eaten it, and stunned that at some time during their meal they had abandoned their caution about poisons or spells. But nothing had happened except for twinges from her overstuffed belly.

'Want to dance?' William stood, and without waiting for an answer took her hand and kissed it, leading her to a small space between the sofas.

She thought briefly about continuing their journey through the labyrinth, but when he pulled her into his arms she felt warm, and she let herself drift into the soft, pulsating rhythms. She fell into step with his gentle swaying. The music swelled and the pools of light within the chamber dimmed, making way for the glow of slowly strobing colours.

They rocked and turned in each other's arms, so close that their heartbeats fell into rhythm with each other, and in turn with the beat of the music that seemed to flow out of the walls.

Small thoughts flicked through Vreni's mind, but before she could make sense of them they flittered out of her awareness again. She could only see William, and only hear the pulse of the music.

They were bathed in the swirls of sparkling coloured light reflected from a mirrored ball that hung high in the domed ceiling. As they danced, William ran his hand across her shoulder and lightly up her neck and into her hair. He leaned towards her and kissed her softly.

Not here. Not in this place.

The thought twisted up into Vreni's mind like steam rising from hot coffee, but then it faded and was gone, leaving her to return to her music and sink her face into William's shoulder. They danced. They kissed.

Not now. They're waiting; Rita's waiting.

'We shouldn't leave Rita sitting on her own,' she whispered into William's ear. She turned and saw Rita lying sleeping on the sofa.

'Rita's not here, it's just us,' he whispered back.

She looked over her shoulder again; the sofa was empty. 'But—of course, it's just us.'

She felt hints of something within her mind, but they were somehow hidden in a mist. She kept dancing and tried to sing along with the music, but each time she did the beat became arrhythmic and the words slipped, turning into something else, as though two songs were being played at the same time.

She shrugged and stopped trying, stopped thinking. 'I could dance with you forever,' she said.

'I'd like that,' William mumbled, squeezing her closer.

She felt something bump her from behind. 'Sorry,' she said automatically.

'How clumsy of us,' said a couple as they dancing past.

She snapped her head around, finally alert to the fact that things weren't right. She saw an old couple. No, she saw an old William and an old Vreni. *What's happening? What is this place?*

The music had faded a little, just for a moment, and she heard other sounds above the melody, voices singing and chanting. The sisters.

The chamber grants your wishes Vreni, Anna said loudly. *It tempts you, and entangles you in trivial desires like picnics and dancing, until that's all you can see.*

'What?' Vreni shook her head again. She felt confused.

The music in the room rose up once more, filling her mind. She leaned into the welcoming warmth of William's body.

Anna called urgently: *Look into the shadows. Open your eyes, Vreni, and see into the shadows.*

For a moment Vreni rested her chin on William's shoulder and peered into the indigo pools of shadow at the edges of the room. She couldn't see anything so she tried again to ignore the insistent voices, but the chanting grew louder, blocking out the dance music.

Anna's voice was unrelenting: *Focus, Vreni, look harder.*

Vreni slowly rocked and waited for her eyes to adjust. She concentrated on the darkened pockets of the room. She thought the dim light and her fatigue were playing tricks on her vision. How could she be seeing what she was seeing?

Reluctantly she slid out of William's arms and walked into the darkness. Lying alone in the gloom was a skeleton. It looked like someone had sat down in the darkness and simply stopped living.

Vreni explored the other puddles of shadow and found two more reclining piles of bones. Each was draped with remnants of rotting clothing, but one also wore a heavy chain that was entangled in its ribs. On the chain hung a silver disc engraved with a spiral.

Vreni knew that pendants like these were worn by some of the Sisters. Her mind cleared instantly, as though a storm wind had blown through it.

Anna sobbed. *Ilona, she said. A sister lost is now found.*

Vreni looked around her. The coloured lights that had seemed so real a moment ago were fading. The music was fading away with it. She felt confused, foolish.

What is your true desire, Vreni? Anna asked urgently. *Keep that desire foremost in your mind and it will give you the strength you need for this battle.*

Vreni wondered how this could be a battle.

We all have to battle false desires in this life, Vreni. What is your true desire? Anna repeated.

Vreni saw images of home and family flash through her mind. She remembered her desire to get the potion and free them. As those thoughts slipped through her mind one by one, they also appeared around her in the chamber.

The smiling faces of Rita and Mama, and the aunties. Papa appeared sitting on the sofa and disappeared again in a flash. Even the ponies flickered briefly into being before fading away.

The glistening bottle that held the sleeping-death potion sat temptingly close on the wooden chest. She lunged for the bottle and grabbed it. She waited for the dread to creep through the glass and seep up her arm, but there was nothing. It wasn't real; none of this was real.

She watched as one desire after another appeared to tempt her, but with each new illusion, the realisation solidified. Her true heart's desire was freedom for herself and her family.

Finally understanding the nature of the chamber, Vreni experimented to see if she could control what was happening. She thought of Rita, and Rita appeared. She thought of the ponies, and they appeared, tossing their heads and whinnying. Then Papa, just once more.

Now that she was sure the chamber would manifest her wishes, she focused her mind on her true desire for freedom and to make her own choices. It was the nature of this chamber to grant her desires and, seeing as her greatest desire was for freedom, it seemed that the chamber was releasing her.

Her head cleared and the confusion of the false visions dissipated.

William reached to offer his embrace again. She shoved him away, trying to bring him to his senses. He came towards her again. At least she knew without doubt now how he truly felt about her and that it wasn't just the magical work of the Sisters that made him have feelings for her.

'William,' she yelled, 'we have to leave.'

'But everything we need is here, and I have you,' he said softly.

Vreni groaned, feeling the frustration growing towards her lovestruck companion. 'We have to go,' she repeated, shoving him again.

Anna's voice came again: *Use his affection for you, Vreni, if that's all he has to offer you right now.*

Vreni pulled on the crimson ribbon and looked at the charms. She touched a shiny globe containing three dark brown cloves. *Cloves on the breath and your lover will do your bidding.* Vreni smiled, remembering the afternoons she had spent with the young sisters, blending herbs and making tinctures while they all played with the idea of what their new power could do for them.

She took the small ball and placed it in her mouth. It began to dissolve and fell loose from the ribbon. The heady fragrance of cloves filled her mouth and wafted up into her nose. She walked towards William, rising up onto her toes so that when she spoke he would breathe in her exhaled words. Then her every whim would be a command to his ears.

'We need to go. I'm leaving and I don't want to leave without you. We have to go *now*.' She pulled him by the arm.

He stared at her and followed, then hesitated. 'But ... we could dance.' He turned back towards the sofas.

She tugged harder, but he was frozen in place, eyes glazed. 'Now,' Vreni implored. She couldn't believe he might choose these trifling pleasures over her. 'We're going. Move!' she screamed, heaving him behind her.

He was like a dead man, shuffling as she dragged him along. They had nearly entered the passageway when the lights dimmed to create pools of colour and the music lifted again. William stopped in mid-step and swayed. He pulled against Vreni, trying to turn back again.

Last Turn

When the songs of the Sisters fill your ears
and your heart you are never alone. So
sing and join with the magic of the music.
Our power is borne on the song.
~ Pratigs Māsa, *Book of Wisdoms*

She yanked William's arm fiercely towards her. Letting go of her frustrations, she punched him hard in the stomach. He let out a groaning breath. She used the last of the strength given to her from her frustration, tightened her grip on his arm, and at last managed to haul him from this strange chamber of desires.

They stumbled down the curving passageway. As she dragged him along, William trudged in a mist, mumbling about food and dancing. Her legs felt as though they were made of stone.

Memories from the chamber remained, and her emotions, a mixture of homesickness and heartbreak, overwhelmed her. The images of her family in the chamber had seemed so real. Apart from when her brother Peters had died and now the unthinkable loss of Papa, she had not felt such a sense of loss as this since she was small and sat next to her sleeping mother, lonely for her to wake up and take her in her arms.

Right now the feelings that the chamber had conjured were holding onto her like an anchor. She had used all her strength to make herself move from the room, and now, along with the weight of remembered sadness, she carried the burden of a dazed William.

She lumbered along the anticlockwise corridor, William shuffling awkwardly behind her like a mindless zombie. The chamber of desires was consumed by the curve of the passageway. The further she got from the turning point, the lighter her legs felt and the clearer her thoughts became, more controlled. She hoped the lingering power of the chamber was leaving William, too, but he continued to shuffle on unchanged.

'So, do you feel like dancing?' she joked, hoping it might break William's zombie-like state. Nothing.

She continued pulling him forward, looking back at him every few steps. She wasn't sure what she was watching for, but checking every few metres became a rhythm, her gaze alternating from him to the stone floor. She trudged on along the curving passageway, her resentment towards William building with each step.

'Vreni, watch it!'

She turned quickly to face William and could see that his eyes were bright and wide, but looking past her up the passageway. He pulled her to an abrupt stop just as she ran into the wall. They had reached another turning already. This one had no challenge, thankfully, as she hadn't even realised where they were.

'Are you all right?' William hugged her, rubbing her shoulders and checking to see if she was hurt. 'You must have tuned out. You need to be more careful.'

'Careful?' she snapped at him, her resentment bubbling up. 'Well, Mr Careful, what was the last thing you remember?' She shoved him in the chest with both hands, letting her frustration resurface.

'What do you mean, remember? You washed my face and we … walked here.' William blinked rapidly, realising something was missing and trying to recall his recent memories.

Vreni stayed angry. She wanted to be alone. She wanted to be up in her tower staring out at the sea. Even now, everything about her life was controlled by someone else. She wanted to be able to make her own choices, and now this frightening place, filled with unspeakable dangers, was probably going to kill her and she wouldn't get a chance to have any life at all or make any choices except the one that had bought her here.

Her eyes burned with the tears of frustration. *How much more of a price am I going to have to pay before I get some control over my own life?*

She turned away from William and stormed off around the turn, veering clockwise again, almost running. Her tears flowed. She felt like screaming; her throat was ropey with the effort of keeping the scream from getting out.

If there had been some way out of this place, she would have slammed through the door and run, and kept running. If she fell into long-sleep then so be it, let some curious scientist slice her open like they'd nearly done to Rita. Then it would all be over, all the complications and secrets no longer her concern. She stomped on, mumbling her tearful frustrations under her breath.

You're doing a difficult thing, Vreni, Anna said soothingly. *And this is the most difficult part of a difficult thing. You might not see your Sisters standing with you, but please believe us when we tell you that you are not alone.*

Vreni's ears filled with the hum of many sweet voices; the chanting was deep and rhythmic, slowing her angry heart. The harmonies surrounded her and for a while she felt enclosed by the music; protected. The enchanted sounds flowed through her, washing away her fierce frustration.

Her tears finally dried to salt on her cheeks. When the music faded, Vreni wiped her eyes and sighed deeply. She realised two things at almost the same time.

The first was that she did not want her life to be over, to be sliced up or any other thing. She was glad she had been chosen and given the chance to make such a change, to bring freedom for her family and for herself. Her life had already changed because of this, and that was worth the fear and the danger. She was one of many strong women. She could feel that inside herself now.

The second realisation came to her in slow stages. She had been almost running along this passageway and she had not reached another turning point yet. This curve was longer than any of the others so far, which meant it must be the last and most outward ring of the labyrinth.

She stopped, breathing hard, and looked back. Shocked, she realised there were doors on the left-hand wall. Those doors must open into the windowed rooms they had seen from the outside of the building. Thankfully there had been no one to notice them as they walked through the passageway. The building still appeared to be empty of people.

The next turn was up ahead. It must be the last turn and after that, they would turn towards the centre of the labyrinth and the vault that contained AlGuild's most precious possessions, one of which had to be the potion.

She stood listening to her heart pounding. She tried to imagine the view from her tower, looking out over the tranquil sea. The imagined scene only calmed her heart a little.

'I'm sorry,' William said, walking up behind her. 'Whatever happened, I left you alone back there.'

'I wasn't alone,' she said, lifting the string of charms the Sisters gave her and rubbing them gently. 'It's all right. It wasn't your fault.'

She told him what had happened in the chamber of desires, or at least what she was clear about in her own mind. He looked bewildered and embarrassed. She checked the bandage she had fashioned from her scarf and saw that it was still in place. It covered more than half his face.

'Are you my mummy?' she smiled, kissing him lightly on his uninjured cheek. 'This is the last turn, you know.'

She leaned flat against the wall, wishing she could push herself through the stone and vanish. What next? What was waiting in the vault?

Anna's voice came to her quietly: *You, Sister Veronika, have come further through the labyrinth than any of us have ever done before. If someone is in the vault you will face great danger. If it is unoccupied, then fortune is smiling on you, but either way we're sure that what you see in there will be disturbing beyond measure. We have witnessed what those in the Alķimķi Ģilde have put their evil hands to over the centuries. We have no reason to think that what lies inside the centre of the labyrinth will be anything less than the full measure of their capabilities.*

The Vault

*AlGuild assures that the highest ethical
standards are met in regard to production.
All our clients can be confident that none
of our products are tested on animals.*
~ AlGuild guide to consumer information

Vreni gulped a breath, but her lungs felt frozen along with the rest of her.

Anna continued speaking: *All your Sisters are with you. You have our charms, and they contain the spirit and sacrifice of every one of us. The amulets allow you to use the power of the earth to impose your intentions. The power is yours, Vreni. You will be able to achieve what is truly your heart's desire. If that weren't true you would already be lost to us, dead or insane. Stand fast, gather your magic and be in control. Victory will be yours. That is your purpose.*

Behind Anna's voice, Vreni could hear the Sisters singing. She knew they were weaving songs of strength and protection. She stood tall. She had chosen to do this, and it was what she had wanted: a chance to change things.

She felt tired and frightened, but she would not be a sleeping princess anymore. She laughed to herself.

'Time to go,' she said, touching the remaining charms that hung around her neck.

'What did they say?' William said, pointing to her ear.

'They said it would be dangerous, and frightening.'

'And what should we do?'

'Think quick, move fast.' She shrugged and smiled, thinking she sounded like an actor from an adventure movie.

'Okay, boss,' William said, giving a mock salute.

They walked the last few metres of the curving passageway and then turned right. The floor sloped downwards. Now the passageway looked older; it was more worn and uneven, like the stone floors in the alchemist's room in Vreni's grandmother's palace.

The rough downward passage stopped at a heavy wooden door. On the door was a strange symbol.

'Silver,' William said. Vreni looked puzzled, so he explained. 'It's an old alchemical symbol for silver. My father likes to collect old drawings. One like this and a few others similar to it hung on a wall at home. I hope this picture's not telling us that this is where they keep their treasure.'

'It depends on what they consider treasure.' She reached out and touched the door handle. It felt cold but smooth, as though worn down by countless hands over the ages. She hesitated.

William's hand came to rest on hers. They turned the handle together and slowly pushed the door inward. It moved with unexpected ease and silence.

The space inside was much larger than Vreni had expected. It was dimly lit by a round skylight at the centre of the high-domed roof, which was letting in the weak glow. The sky outside looked like late afternoon, but Vreni had lost track of how long they had been travelling through the labyrinth.

The room was circular, as she had expected, with high walls that were lined with shelves full of books and bottles and small chests. In between the banks of shelves, oil paintings hung in heavy gold and silver frames. There was a scattering of furniture. There were reading tables holding heavy leather-bound volumes, stiff-backed chairs and some low divans with rich velvet coverlets.

There was a raised platform in the centre of the room, directly under the light-filled dome. On the platform sat a large, gnarled tree. The tree was bare of leaves, as it would appear in autumn, although Vreni thought this one could be bare because it was old, its sap had dried up, and it was no longer able to sustain leaves or fruit.

She scanned the room more carefully now. She was thinking of the alchemist's room in her grandmother's palace, and the wolf that was held there and set loose to kill her. She didn't see any obvious sign of guards or defence, but then she saw something she could barely believe.

Her face flushed with an awful heat as she gazed upon three young girls. They were the same girls she had seen when she visited the dream realm, she was sure of it. The girls lay now as they had back then, heaped together on a low divan. They looked as though they were simply sleeping, but Vreni recognised them, and that meant they had been held by the sleeping-death for centuries.

She shuddered. These girls had been stolen away from their families and robbed of their lives, and were now imprisoned in the darkness at the edge of death. This would have been her grandmother's fate if it hadn't been for the Wise Sisters.

Wordlessly she squeezed William's arm and pointed. She walked towards the girls, scanning the darker places in the vault as she moved, half expecting some creature to leap at her from its hiding place.

She knelt beside the girls' wretched bed and brushed a gentle hand across their young faces. Their faces were soft, and so still, held slightly out of time. She felt like she had when she would sneak into Rita and Mama's bedrooms to spend time with them when she was very lonely.

Seeing the girls again, feeling their dusty hair and the brittleness of the cloth of their dresses, rotten with age, Vreni was fuelled with determination. She was so close to changing all this. She touched the vial of softening potion hanging with her other charms.

'I could free them now,' she whispered.

There'll be time for that later, Anna said.

'But if—'

Faith, Vreni.

'Yes.' She knew Anna was right. Why wake them now to face who knew what?

Vreni stood and moved towards the shelves to seek out the remaining sleeping-death potion. The Sisters had been sure that even a few drops would be enough for them to create a formula to fully reverse the curse and save Vreni, her family, and maybe, somehow, the sleeping girls. She was so close now.

Standing in the dim shadows cast across the shelves, Vreni tried to reach out with her mind, to sense the potion. Its resonance had been gouged deep into her awareness when she touched it in the dream realm. She could still recall the cold dread that had seeped through the glass, and the feel of the terrible icy darkness that had crawled across her skin, as if the liquid inside the bottle were trying to find a place to enter her body. She searched through the shelves, reaching out with her awareness.

William moved around the tree on the pedestal, trying to find a better position from which to watch over her more closely.

On the third bank of shelves Vreni was instinctively drawn to an ornate silverbox that was high up and almost out of reach. She opened it and removed the small, familiar bottle from its bed of decaying red velvet. As she lifted the thick glass of the bottle she felt the haunting cold rise up her arm, but this time the feeling of dread was mixed with relief. This was it. It would all be over soon.

There was a soft, rustling sound behind her. She jumped and the bottle fell from her hand, rolling away across the knotted wooden bench. At the edge of her vision she saw something move. Both she and William turned towards the central platform. It seemed as though the old, half-dead tree had moved.

'What was that?' she asked.

'I think it moved,' William said.

'The tree?'

'Maybe not.' Now he sounded doubtful.

Then a ripple of movement ran through the tree once more. William moved toward Vreni protectively.

The fading light in the room made it difficult for them to see the tree in any detail. It was swollen and stump-like, with only two branches reaching feebly towards the domed ceiling. One of the branches had sprouted an unusual taproot that trailed down and joined with the floor.

The tree didn't look as though it was planted in any soil. Its swollen roots seemed to spread out across the platform and disappear under a thick blanket of mouldering leaves, which lay all around it, cushioning its bulk. Resting at the top of the trunk, between the two uplifted branches, was a rounded, wrinkled stump.

The tree was topped with a spray of gnarled twigs sticking out at odd angles, making Vreni think of an ugly head with outstretched arms, but then all trees looked a bit like that, she decided, especially in winter.

The trunk of the tree was bulbous and distorted. It looked as though it was collapsing in on itself. The bark was murky and uneven. It warped and folded to accommodate the crooked shapes.

'I must've been seeing things,' William said quietly, and he turned back again to the job of scanning the room.

The tree shuddered once again, and the arm-branches stiffened, the tree's trunk appeared to swell and collapse again, and what sounded like a loud breath was somehow exhaled from it.

Vreni and William stared transfixed as two eyes blinked open in the bark, which was now turning into a face on a stumpy wooden head resting limply on the right branch-arm. A small twisted mouth opened with a rasping yawn. Clearly visible were the features of the face within the crinkled folds of bark.

Glassy eyes the colour of autumn leaves stared out from their woody sockets. The eyes looked around without seeming to focus on anything. The branches rustled feebly again and Vreni realised that this was the face and arms, and the swollen curves of an old female body. Any legs that may once have existed had long ago been transformed into roots. This thing was made from wood, or had been turned into wood, but either way it had to be the work of the alchemists and their organisation, AlGuild.

'What is that?' William asked.

'*Who* is that, you mean. What have they done to her, and how?'

'She's beautiful, isn't she?' said a deep, viscous voice from somewhere in the darkness.

Vreni felt her heart thump up into her throat. Her ears buzzed with the rush of blood as her heart pounded violently.

'Captivating,' added the unseen voice.

William was frozen in place. His face was the colour of stone. He was staring intently into the patch of darkness where the voice had come from.

'Can you see anything?' Vreni said.

'I think my mind's still playing tricks from before. I'm sure that's all it is, it can't be—anything else,' William whispered, and shook his head slowly, stiffly.

His breath shuddered and his shoulders hunched forward. He stared down, as if looking through the floor at something no one else could see. Rubbing the key amulet between his fingers, he turned to look at Vreni and his eyes were wet. He squeezed the key, digging it hard into his palm.

'What is it, William?' she whispered.

Leave it alone, Vreni, Anna said. *He can't say the words yet, not even to himself.*

'What words?'

You'll know later, Anna said firmly.

Vreni wished she knew what was going on.

'I like to watch her sleeping,' came the voice from the darkness. 'I wait for her to wake, longing to see those sparkling amber eyes.'

Vreni squeezed her trembling hands into fists; now there were footsteps coming from where William had been staring.

Lights flickered on around the room. A tall gaunt man, more bone than flesh, walked slowly towards them, never once taking his eyes off the wooden woman on the platform. The bony man wore a look of love and longing that Vreni had sometimes seen on her father when he thought he was alone, sitting with his sleeping wife.

The strange thin man's gaze never faltered. He moved close to them and then walked past, appearing spellbound. He stepped up onto the platform and brushed his fingers tenderly across the rough, bark-encrusted cheek of the reclining figure.

'My Rozālija, I am here. I'll be here for you always,' he murmured.

William was shaking. His eyes were wide open and staring. His jaw was clenched.

Vreni came closer to William, trying to offer some comfort. This man seemed more frightening to him than anything else so far. What was it about him that had William in such a state? Right now she had no chance of finding out.

She took William's hand and squeezed it. 'I don't think he sees us,' she whispered.

'Yes, I see you,' the man said without taking his eyes off the Rozālija creature. 'As master of the guild, I have many ways of seeing and a plethora of other useful skills. And after I have gazed into the eyes of my love I will show you some of those skills—by killing you both.'

The words echoed in Vreni's head. Her hands shook as she played nervously with the amulets hanging around her neck. She could feel their power tingling against her skin.

You know about your grandmother's aunts, Vreni, Anna said. They were all named for the most beautiful flowers. They were the first of the Wise Sisters, and Rozālija was the one that plotted with the alchemists to kill Ieva. We heard rumours that the alchemists had somehow used the sleeping-death potion to keep the old witch alive. It's hard to believe she's endured so long, and now she's this—barely human thing.

'This is Veca Tante?'

'Yes,' the Master said. 'Some people used to call her that, so long ago. Never us, never her loyal Alķimķi Ģilde, but others, the witches, her sisters.' He paused and stroked the bark-encrusted face as if offering comfort. 'They told their stories and kept telling them until the world believed she was an ugly old witch. But as you can see they were all just stories. She is glorious. She is beautiful.' He leaned in slowly and kissed the wooden cheek with surreal gentleness.

The words the Master spoke filled Vreni's mind with an icy fog. She couldn't think what action to take. This really was Veca Tante. This wizened enchantress who had kept men imprisoned generation after generation, making them do her bidding. This husk of a man was her devoted servant.

Is Veca Tante really still waiting for the day when she'll defeat the Wise Sisters? Does she even know who she was, or what she's become?

Vreni had always thought of herself as some kind of freak for being a sleeper, but now she realised she wasn't a monster at all.

Vreni looked past Veca Tante to where the three girls were sleeping. She had heard what Anna said, but all she could think of was that if she was going to die today then she would at least release these three girls from their prison first. She started to move around the platform. Her fingers found the small vial of softening formula hanging among the charms. She edged towards the sleeping girls.

With incomprehensible speed the Master drew himself from his adoring trance and moved to block her path.

'You are a sister-witch,' he snarled. He leaned horribly close, his face briefly brushing her skin, and sniffed her. 'No, you are a sleeper. Are you one of Ieva's daughters, a granddaughter? No matter, you will be just as dead, whoever you are.'

He leaned over her and sniffed her face once more. 'Rozālija was right to believe the whispers about the sleepers and the sister-witches. How curious and delightful to see one of you after all these years, but you leave our little experiment alone.'

'Experiment!' Vreni exploded. 'This is *not* an experiment. These girls were someone's daughters. You fiends and that *creature* might have had some ludicrous motive for doing what you did to my grandmother, but why these girls? They offered no advantage to your—*cause*.' The word was like acid on her tongue.

The Master moved back again to touch his beloved Rozālija.

Vreni edged closer to the sleeping girls. She felt a cold grip on her legs, freezing her in mid-step. She couldn't move. She felt as though there was a band of ice around her neck. Her throat was constricted and she pressed against the invisible, frozen collar, trying to loosen it.

'Now, now, young witch, the Alķimķi Ģilde didn't just play with daba like your sister-witches do. Your Pratigs Māsa'—

he spat out the words—'spent their time dancing around with nature and making magic to soften and manipulate, trying to do good.'

He flicked one hand and bunches of herbs lifted off the benches and flew into the air, whirling above their heads. 'The Alķimķi Ģilde uses magic as a science.' He gestured again, and this time a few leather-bound books lifted to join the swirling throng. 'We needed to have scientific rigor.' He sounded manic and patronising. 'All good science has to have sound experimental practice in place. These girls were simply an experiment—'

A strangled murmur came from the platform. The Master stopped and turned his gaze once again on the tree-witch.

Vreni felt the grip on her legs and throat release, and the floating objects dropped abruptly to the floor. She lunged towards the girls again, but somehow the old man was there to block her way. He leaned down and scooped up one of the girls with a single arm, obviously much stronger than he appeared. The girl hung there like a rag doll.

'We don't think of these specimens as actual people,' he said. 'We consider them to be useful laboratory rats, nothing more, and I'll still have two left.' He took a knife from his belt and plunged it into the girl's chest.

Vreni flinched. She felt the contents of her stomach rising into her mouth and swallowed hard. She waited for some reaction from the rag-doll girl; how could she not feel the knife in her chest, in her heart? But the girl just hung in the man's arms, undisturbed. No blood came from her wound. Vreni struggled to accept that this could be happening.

The Master casually dropped the girl back onto the divan with the knife still poking up from the fabric of her dress.

Suddenly the Master's bony hand took hold of Vreni, wrapping tightly around her neck. William raced to help her, but was snared mid-step by the Master's invisible choke collar. He stood gasping for breath, struggling to reach her.

She pushed at the attacking arm, trying to get him to release her. She thumped and scratched, feeling the hard muscles flexing as his hand constricted around her throat. She felt crunching in her neck as he squeezed. Pain radiated through her jaw and up into her ears. Her lungs heaved uselessly as she struggled for air. A thunderous buzzing-ringing filled her ears, and patches of wild, fizzing colour blocked her vision.

The Master's face was so close to hers. He stared into her widening eyes.

'I have lots of dramatic ways to kill you,' he whispered, 'but I do enjoy the, um, personal touch.'

With the last of her energy, she kicked out at his legs and slammed her fists into the sides of his chest as hard as she could. He wrenched her off her feet. She could feel the weight of her body pulling on her neck as she dangled. As she struggled, she reached toward the divan with one foot, hoping to support her weight.

The pressure on her throat was complete; she had no air. As her world began to blacken and fade she felt the Master's face touching hers.

'I like to collect last breaths,' he snickered quietly. 'I like to inhale the last breath a person will ever breathe. I have quite a collection.'

William moved again. The old man was too enthralled by the sight of Vreni dying to think about keeping him under control.

As though she was a precious object, the Master moved Vreni almost gently towards the divan to lay her with the others.

The knife! With her last effort Vreni stretched out her chin and bit into the Master's sallow cheek, clamping down with all the strength she had left. She could taste the salty iron of his blood in her mouth. He let out an angry growl, and slowly pulled his dagger out of the rag-doll girl. It came away clean.

'You're harder to kill than I expected,' he said. 'How delightful.'

Vreni felt his hot whisper in her ear. She saw the knife, held high. Then she saw William's reflection glinting in the metal of the blade.

There was a heavy grunt as air was expelled from the Master's lungs. Vreni wobbled as he regained his footing, and now she could feel the floor under her feet again. William's arm came up underneath the hand that held the knife, smashing the blade free of the Master's grip. It tumbled through the air and landed with a quiet snick of metal cutting flesh. Vreni dreaded to think which girl had been stabbed now.

The constriction around her neck was released and she collapsed to the floor, gasping hungrily for air. She scrambled blindly to get away from the Master, and didn't stop until she collided with one of the wooden shelves. She leaned back, trying to stifle her sobs, panting, trying to focus her blurred vision and clear away the blackness.

The room came slowly into focus. William and the Master were knotted grotesquely together, each gripping the other's throat. William was a full head taller than his emaciated opponent, but the Master was still able to lift him from the floor, as he had done with Vreni. William was planting violent kicks into the Master's legs, which caused the old man to lower him briefly so his feet could touch the floor, offering a precious second to snatch a breath. But William's colour was fading.

Vreni looked around at the malevolence and death in the room, and realised she would have to add to it if this was to be truly finished. *This has to stop.*

She reached for the charms. Finding a small sphere full of frog spawn, she placed it in her hand and whispered to the glass to melt; a moment later minute tadpoles swam around in the dish of her cupped palm. She chanted.

'Swim and grow, swim and grow,'
'You are no longer tiny eggs.
Lose your tails and find your legs.
Seek a hiding place, beyond the tongue,
Keep growing till his life is done.'

She shuddered at the command's intention— *her* intention.

When she had finished chanting, her hand contained seven shiny green frogs. They hopped gently down onto the stone floor and moved unnoticed to where William and the Master were still locked in battle.

William looked determined rather than scared, and he had a look of something else, as though this battle was his. What had he realised that she had not? Vreni whispered her spell again, sending her frogs to obey her commands.

The frogs reached the heels of the Master's shoes. They started to climb up the back of his trousers, growing a little more as they ascended, their sticky footpads clinging to the fabric as they climbed.

William's eyes flickered when he saw them appear at the Master's shoulders. From there the frogs lolloped out along the Master's arms. Stopping at his wrists, they blinked serenely, and waited until the Master opened his mouth to roar another threat at William. Then the creatures leapt into the moist darkness and slipped easily beyond the Master's tongue, down deep into his throat.

The shrivelled man's grip on William loosened. William lifted his knee and rammed it deep into the Master's stomach. The man collapsed onto the floor and lay coughing. William stepped clear of the fallen man's reach and watched as he writhed on the cold stone. The old man's face was making shapes as if he was trying to scream, but no sound came out.

Vreni rose to her feet and walked closer to see the effects of her spell. She knew the frogs would continue to grow to full size inside the Master's throat and block off his airway.

She knew this was happening because it was her intention when she chanted the spell. This was what she had wished for—for the Master to never be able to do harm again. *Is this who I am? A killer? Is this what I need to become to be Veronika, bringer of victory?*

William had become stone-like again. He stared down at the gasping old man.

'What is it?' she asked.

Leave him with his moment, he will tell you when he can, Anna said.

As the two men stared at each other, the Master's body started to spasm and jerk. His chest heaved as his lungs tried desperately to suck air through his amphibian-filled throat. He grabbed at his neck, trying to swallow. His sallow face turned grey. His lips turned blue, then a deeper blue again. His eyes bulged with the effort of trying to breathe.

Then his eyes could no longer stare at William. The dilated irises rolled upwards under his fast-blinking eyelids until they were gone forever, leaving just the yellow-white of his eyeballs, traced with a web of tiny red lines formed by bursting blood vessels. The Master's body heaved and arched. His hands clenched and unclenched, and his feet kicked out weakly at nothing.

Then everything was still. The old man lay on the dark stone floor like a bony blue ghost. The frogs had completed their task.

'What happened just then?' Vreni asked William.

'Tell you later,' he mumbled.

The Master and Veca Tante are a team, Anna said forcefully. *You need to act on the old witch as well. Soften her, Vreni. Use the vial.*

'But what about the girls?'

We can help the girls later, but take action against Tante now or we may still lose it all.

Softening

*All things that are begun will end. All
things that are made will be unmade and
remade to begin again. Then are beginnings
endings or endings beginnings?*

~ Pratigs Māsa, *Book of Questions*

Vreni took the vial of green liquid from around her neck and jumped onto the leaf-strewn platform. Veca Tante made distressed mewing sounds as her eyes darted around the room, searching for her ensorcelled lover, and then they fixed on Vreni.

Do those yellow cat-eyes truly see me? How alive is she inside her wooden prison?

Vreni caught sight of the heavy silver spiral amulet hanging around the thick, inhuman neck. *How dare you wear the sign of the Pratigs Māsa?* Vreni gripped the pedant and yanked at it, snapping the ancient chain. Veca Tante let out an anguished cry.

Vreni broke open the small vial of softening formula and poured its syrupy contents onto the rough bark skin. It dribbled into the folds of the witch's distorted cleavage and soaked quickly into her woody flesh. Veca Tante quivered, and a low gargling growl came from between her bark-covered lips.

Vreni shoved the old witch's amulet into her pocket and jumped down from the platform. She returned to William, who was still standing over the Master's fallen body. The blue lips twitched and rippled, and Vreni felt her heart gallop again. Surely he couldn't still be alive.

But no, the dead cheeks fluttered and the thin lips grimaced into a morbid smile as the frogs squirmed their way back out of their victim's mouth. One by one, the emerald frogs appeared through the Master's thin, blue lips. They glistened in the softening light of the room. All seven frogs remained on the dead face, their large eyes looking around, blinking slowly. They began to croak quietly.

Vreni reached out to William. He turned slowly from the face full of frogs to look at her. He appeared to thaw slightly.

From behind them there was groaning and wailing. They turned and watched as Veca Tante twitched and shuddered. Wordless noises, full of grief, came from her wooden lips. She sobbed as pieces of her crusty bark skin flaked away and fell to the platform.

There was a dull thud. They both jumped and turned to see that a small piece of decorative wood panelling had fallen to the stone floor. Their eyes tracked upwards to see where it had come from. The timber that panelled the ceiling was splitting and breaking apart. The domed-glass skylight began to sputter and crack as the ceiling warped.

Glass started to rain down across the platform, and needle-like shards pierced the tender flesh that had been exposed as the old witch's bark fell away. Now she howled and contorted.

The cracks opening up and down her body oozed a mucky-brown sap. Ripples ran across her wooden body, which undulated from the roots pushing the remaining sap upwards. With each pumping wave, the brown fluid oozed more freely from the cracks and wounds as it made its way to her head and moved up into the stunted branches that might once have been her hair. These thin branches sprouted tiny dots of green that budded with unnatural speed. Shining green leaves uncurled and grew. Buds appeared and swelled, and when they opened the flowers bloomed: here a daisy, there something that looked like mistletoe, and some chicory flowers. Last of all, one perfect red rose grew and threw open its petals.

'It's as though she knows this is her end,' Vreni said to William. 'All plants feel the harshness of winter coming and know they could die in the snow. She's setting seed. Seeds are the immortality of the forest.'

'Yes, this is her end,' William agreed. Look.'

As the bark fell away, soft spaces of flesh were left bare, filling quickly with a squirming sea of worms and beetles.

'She's doing what old trees should do,' Vreni said, almost reverently. 'She's composting and returning to the earth.'

The beetles and worms roiled over one another, feasting on the mushy wooden flesh. They multiplied and spilled out over the edge of the bark and flowed across the trembling body. Veca Tante opened and closed her mouth, but she no longer made sounds. A quivering wave of tiny creatures crawled across the old witch's face and entered her mouth and eyes. With one last shudder, she shook her head fiercely and crumpled. Her large bloated body sagged and collapsed inwards, pulling the face and the stunted arms down to form a pile of disintegrating humus.

All that remained on top of the rotting pile was the rose, the last three petals clinging to its red rosehip, which was swollen with seeds.

'It smells like the forest.' Vreni breathed deeply.

A second heavy wooden panel crashed down to their right. The ceiling was buckling and cracking open.

This place was held together by the old witch's magic, Anna said.

Vreni looked up, surprised to see the first traces of faint early-morning light glowing through the cracks in the roof. Another panel fell. Above it, the metal of the exterior roof screeched as it twisted.

'We have to get out of here.' William pointed to a door that had not been visible before. He pulled Vreni in that direction.

'Not without the girls.'

She shook off his grip and ran back around the platform to the dusty divan. She lifted the wounded girl into her arms. She felt as light as a baby bird. Beside her, William knelt and lifted the other two girls with a grunt, laying one over each shoulder.

They turned towards the door. Another piece of the ceiling crashed down, falling across Vreni's shoulder. Her skin burned as the wood grazed its way down her back. A jagged nail sliced open the back of her heel.

'We have to get to the door,' William said. 'The roof won't last much longer.'

Around them the roof beams groaned, and heavy wooden panels peeled away from the walls like old bark. Sheets of metal swung from the disintegrating roof.

They zigzagged through the debris and finally reached the door. William walked through, but Vreni hesitated.

'Come on,' he said.

He laid the two girls down and turned back to help her. He took the wounded girl and started to pull Vreni through into the short and incredibly narrow passageway. She could see morning light coming through the door at the other end.

'No!' she yelled above the whining of the twisting roof metal.

She ran back into the crumbling room, circling to the right. She stayed close to the wall to gain some protection from the falling roof. Reaching the shelves where she had found the velvet-lined box, she remembered that the bottle had rolled from her grasp when Veca Tante had startled her. She quickly checked the bench where she thought it had gone, but it wasn't there. Throwing herself down on the floor, she thrust her arm under the bottom of the cabinet and groped wildly.

Her hand landed on the cool glass, and again she felt the creeping cold travelling up her fingers and across her palm. Blessings.

As she pulled the bottle out from under the cabinet, a large wooden beam came loose from the roof with a loud screech. She curled up her body to protect the bottle and its horrible–wonderful contents. The beam struck her back. Most of the beam's weight hit the shelf first, but it knocked the air from her lungs as it slammed into her shoulder and pushed her head into the heavy cabinet door. Her leg was pinned in place by the beam. She was trapped.

The bottle! She rolled it fearfully in her palm and smiled; it was unbroken.

'Vreni!' William called.

'I can't move.'

'On my way.'

There was another crash. The door was now blocked by a second fallen beam, with William on the other side.

'I know I'm not alone,' Vreni said, urging herself to stay calm and remember her powers.

You are never alone, Anna said. *Remember, you have all our love and our strength, always.*

Vreni tucked the precious bottle of sleeping potion into the silk pouch around her neck and felt for the glistening red amulet hanging among the remaining charms.

That contains a drop of blood from each of us at Mežs Mājas, Anna said. *Each drop has travelled through the heart of the Sister who gave it and contains the strength and love of us all.*

Vreni placed the glass bubble, full of blood, onto her tongue and concentrated, remembering the faces of her sisters and the sweetness of their voices as they sang joyfully together. She thought of Rita, her mother, her aunties and the cursed girls, robbed of their lives. The bubble melted away and she tasted the salty-sweet strength on her tongue.

I am Veronika, bringer of victory.

Growing warmth spread throughout her body, and she could her sisters singing. She arched her back, feeling the jagged edges of the wooden beam digging into her skin. She inhaled deeply, smelling the blood of her sisters on her lips. She pushed with the force of many and lifted the beam. She quickly slipped sideways, freeing herself from the trap before it dropped back down.

She threaded her way through the destruction in the vault and back to the blocked door. She leaned her weight against the fallen beam that blocked the doorway and pushed hard. It scraped noisily as it slid slowly across the brass strap that banded the exit.

Vreni could feel the borrowed power from the charm waning. She pulled at the door and managed to open it just enough to squeeze through. The door slammed shut again behind her, knocking into her back. She stumbled towards William, who stood holding the two sleeping girls.

'We have to go *now*,' he urged.

All she could do was nod as she lifted the third girl into her arms. Feeling the last of the borrowed strength seep fully from her now, she leaned on William for a moment while her head spun. She breathed deeply and found a last vestige of strength from the charm.

'Thank you, my Sisters,' she murmured.

They turned and walked quickly down the passageway as the building disintegrated behind them. Pushing open the final door, they walked out into the morning sunshine and away from the collapsing ruins. The sun seemed a ridiculously normal sight after everything that had happened since they had seen it last.

Still watching for danger, Vreni caught sight of the guard standing dazed outside the building. He looked their way, but didn't seem to see them. He turned, as though he had heard something, and walked purposefully away from them, around the side of the building. They walked quickly out the front gate and into the empty carpark.

The guard watched, transfixed, as the building collapsed. He didn't even notice the unauthorised vehicle that entered the carpark, loaded its five passengers, and drove away.

Diminishing

Is it the raindrop that makes the flood?
Does an egg hold the bird's song?
Is the tree hiding within the seed?
		~ Pratigs Māsa, *Book of Questions*

The young security guard stumbled around the buckling metal shell of the building; hour after hour, he circled the outer wall. He listened to the structure inside collapsing and crashing down, but he was listening for another sound as well. He was sure he could hear a cry for help, a plaintive call from beyond the warping steel walls.

He had seen them get out, hadn't he? He thought he remembered seeing someone, but the memory was unclear. All he knew clearly now was that he was needed by someone. He could definitely hear a voice calling—couldn't he?

Plumes of dust rose up with each crash. He walked around the building, tugging at each buckling window in turn. He slammed his fists against the glass, hoping he could break them. Each time he passed the front door he tried the security pad. Nothing. He slammed his shoulder hard against the door until he felt dizzy. Nothing.

He circled in this way throughout the day; swooning each time he heard a whisper of voice from beyond the bent walls. At sunset he discovered a place where the twisting metal had ripped apart, forming a ragged gash in the wall. He tugged at the sharp edges. Trickles of blood flowed across his palms. Finally he made the opening wide enough to clamber through. The jagged metal caught on his shoulder as he passed, but the wound went unnoticed.

Within the walls nothing remained except piles of stone and rotting timber. The scene looked like an ancient ruin. He stumbled in and out of the detritus. He could hear the voice all the more strongly now. Its soft words filled his head and his heart.

He came at last to the centre of what used to be the building. The sun was setting and the last light painted the sky orange and red. He knelt among the shards of broken glass, and tenderly reached to pickup what remained of a rose from where it clung to a thin, twisted branch poking up from the rubble.

'You are beautiful, my beautiful rose.'

He held the rose gently in his bloody palm. Its three remaining red velvet petals quivered, and fell loose into his hand. The bulging rosehip shone a vivid crimson. He held the round seed pod to his heart.

'I'm yours, always.'

He stood and stumbled back through the rubble, holding the rosehip lovingly to his heart. Once outside he stared into the darkening red of the setting sun and started walking westward, looking for a place to plant his seeds.

Homecoming

*Home is family and fealty, comfort and
companionship, acceptance and truth.
Home is a palace, a cottage, or a heart.*
~ Pratigs Māsa, *Book of Wisdoms*

As the car dropped down into the green, birch-filled valley of Mežs Mājas, Vreni finally allowed herself to relax. She had tried to whisper questions to Sabina, but her voice must have been too quiet, or Anna was making her wait, and the answers she sought would come later.

Vreni sat with the girls in the back seat of the car while William sat up front with the driver. She wasn't sure if he was really sleeping but that was how it looked; there were no answers from him either.

She rolled down the window and breathed in the cool fragrance of the forest. Home. William stirred in the front seat.

As the curved dirt road bought them closer to the cottages at the centre of the valley, Vreni could see Sisters standing on the verges, smiling and waving. When the car passed, they followed behind like they were joining a parade. The birdsong under the trees was gradually overtaken by the joyous chanting and singing, which intensified as each new voice joined in.

The car circled through the gardens, and as it passed in front of the lab building Vreni saw Sabina and Anna waving and singing among the cluster of happy faces, fully restored and as beautiful and radiant as she had ever seen them.

Now Vreni realised why they hadn't given her any answers on the trip home: the spell had been undone.

She wriggled her shoulder from under the sleeping girls. The car had barely stopped when she pushed open the door, scrambled across the gravel and threw herself at Sabina and Anna. Her legs buckled beneath her. Their arms encircled her tightly and held her weight as she nuzzled into them and let her tears flow. Pressed so closely between the two women, Vreni could feel the vibrations of their humming through her skin. As Sabina cooed quietly, the music surrounded Vreni and she felt her strength returning.

The bottle containing the potion pressed coldly against her skin. She slipped it from around her neck and handed it to Anna, who held the bottle high in the air.

'Veronika, bringer of victory,' Sabina announced.

Everyone cheered and crowded in around her, pulling William into the excited crescendo of celebration until they were standing close together. Vreni's mind swelled with questions again, but in the joyous noise, all she could do was smile and hug him.

'Thank you,' she managed to say as the music and laughter continued.

'Now, I must be indelicate,' Anna said, smiling, 'you two badly need a bath and a change of clothes.'

'Yes,' Sabina agreed. 'You need to clean yourselves up and get some rest, and tonight we'll have a feast in honour of your victory.'

The crowd thinned, and Vreni watched as the sleeping girls were carried into the laboratory.

It was late afternoon when Vreni walked out into the garden. Her bath had been fragrant and energising. She knew the water had been laced with restorative potions, and she was glad of it because she could feel her physical and emotional strength starting to return. The setting sun was painting crimson-orange light across the treetops as she walked slowly through the patchwork of flowerbeds and ponds, heading for the quiet of the pine grove.

Under the green canopy the air became cool and still. As her eyes adjusted to the deep shadows, she saw William. He was sitting down, leaning against the rough bark of one of the older trees. He looked refreshed and his wounds were covered with clean white dressings.

'Do you come here often?' she said, trying to sound cheerful although she was bursting with questions.

'I do.' He smiled. 'They have a great light show and the girls are great dancers.' He stood up and bowed dramatically. 'Will you dance with me?'

'How could I resist?'

They curled into each other's arms and started to sway slowly.

'We did it,' she whispered, and felt his arms grow suddenly tense around her. Realising he wasn't going to say anything yet, she let it go. 'You're right, it is a great light show here.'

His arms relaxed and they danced until the light faded.

William led her out of the pine grove to the wooden bench by the pond. The light from the buildings created a shimmering patchwork on the still surface of the water. The noise of happy preparations echoed from the cottage windows.

Vreni softly touched the dressed wounds on William's face. 'I can't thank you enough for what you've done for me. I wouldn't have been victorious, or even alive now, if you hadn't been there.'

'You're welcome, but like I said before we entered the labyrinth, I was doing this for me too. I wanted some freedom, and now —' He trailed off. He was rubbing the key amulet between his fingers.

'You don't need that key anymore,' she said.

'I never needed it, Vreni.'

'I don't understand?'

'It was a bio-lock, set to a DNA pattern.'

'But the key overrode the lock, otherwise only the Master could open it.'

William took a deep breath and held it for a moment. 'Or someone with very similar DNA.'

'I still don't understand.'

'The Master is, was, my father,' he whispered.

Vreni felt her throat tighten. 'What? That can't be true.'

'I know my own father's face,' he said slowly.

'You knew when you saw him inside the vault. Why didn't you tell me?' Hot tears rolled down her cheeks.

'Because when I saw that it was him, suddenly everything made horrible sense. I realised what he must have done to my sister and to my mother. He needed a son to follow in his footsteps. Once he had that—' William shuddered and released an anguished sigh.

'You should have told me,' she choked out.

'How could I have said that to you, Vreni? It made no sense to me, I could barely admit it to myself.'

'But if I'd known—' She was trembling.

'If you had known, could you have done what you did?'

'I killed your father.'

The words crackled like lightning. She felt dizzy and couldn't breathe. Knowing she had ended the life of a cruel, half-human monster, a stranger, was bad enough, but now this anonymous stranger had become a person. *I have killed a person.*

'I'm sorry, but I needed you to do what you did. I *wanted* you to kill him. It had to happen for you and your family, but also for me, and for my mother. I believe he killed her once he had me to groom to one day take his place. He would have made sure I was held under the witch's spell, to be the next master. The alchemists made prisoners of us both. He was a monster, Vreni, he was never my father.'

Vreni pushed away from William and retreated to a tree at the edge of the pine grove. She pressed her face hard into the rough bark. An angry storm of questions brewed in her mind. *Did Sabina know about all this? Why didn't she tell me? Are we just puppets, dangling on the magical strings of the Pratigs Māsa?*

'We haven't been controlling you,' Sabina said quietly behind Vreni. 'We've watched as the succession of masters came and went over the centuries, so we knew who he was, but when you met William that was not our doing. That was your fate, and his. You were meant to meet each other that day. Love is far more powerful than all our magic.'

'You used him,' Vreni growled. 'You brought him here to get what you wanted.'

'When we knew who he was, we realised he could enter the labyrinth undetected, but the choice was always his. Always.'

'So are you really my Sister, my friend, or was that just to get close enough to secretly train me?' Hot tears rolled down her face. 'Did you train me to kill?' She was sobbing. 'And Papa? Did you do that to Papa to make me come with you?' Vreni struggled to breathe.

'I have known your father all my life.' Sabina's tears flowed freely now as well. 'I watched as he guarded you and protected you with all his love. I wished he were my father. I know the pain of your loss.'

Sabina took Vreni in her arms, and Vreni crumpled.

'Please believe me,' Sabina said soothingly. 'We saw the opportunity for real success when fate bought you and William together. But think back over what happened and you'll realise that William's feelings for you are real. Neither of you would have done anything against your will. Seek inside yourself and know that this is true.'

Vreni drew in a purposeful, calming breath as William approached. She looked from one to the other. She saw the truth in their connecting and unfolding stories.

There was the scuffle of gravel as Anna ran from the lab into the cottage; then a loud cheer erupted.

Sabina gripped Vreni's arm. 'That cheering means only one thing, Vreni. The potion will work. There will be a cure. You have done it,' she cried, wrapping her arms around them both. 'Come on, we have a victory to celebrate.' She guided them towards the festivities.

My Soul to Keep

*The sleeping curse gave us purpose, and
made us who we were. The cure has given
us choice and promise, and remade us
into something we are yet to discover.*

~ Pratigs Māsa, *New Book of Wisdoms*

Vreni stood in her tower, staring out to the east, across the sea. The sun was sinking low. The tower cast a long shadow across the garden and out to the edge of the cliff. The sea beyond was turning a deep purple; it would soon be swallowed by night time. A few stars were sprinkled across the evening sky.

Vreni thought of the long ago times in her childhood when she had built rickety playhouses out of worn blankets. The light that penetrated through the holes in the blankets had been her make-believe stars and the moon she had dreamed of visiting. She wished she could still pretend and weave a world made of stories and un-truths, but she had truths now and she had come up here to make the choices she was finally free to make.

There were three truths that Vreni carried with her now. She opened her journal, hoping that her thoughts would become clear as the words tumbled onto the pages. Each sleeper would be offered a cure; she had a decision to make soon.

She wrote: *Truth: I killed a man. I did not hold a knife or brew a poison or shoot a gun, but I made my intentions clear. I wove the magic and gave instructions to the frogs. The frogs didn't kill him; they only did what I instructed them to do, what it was their nature to do—grow and hop and seek out a moist hiding place. I brought them to life and sent them down the Master's throat. I knew what would happen, and I still made it happen.*

Vreni stared out the window and wondered about her own nature.

Truth: I am a magical creature; I live by magical rules. Like Veca Tante, I have used a variation of the sleeping potion to travel through time. She used it wishing to live long enough to defeat us. I have used it and witnessed the wonder of change across my century.

Magic had saved them and imprisoned them all. William was meant to be the next placed under the old witch's spell, to adore her and serve her until he was used up. Isn't that what he would become if he wore her father's silver amulet?

Truth: the Wise Sisters have done what they promised and reversed the sleeping potion. Now all sleepers have a choice. When Rita, Mama and the aunties next wake they can choose to take the formula and be free. The new formula has worked, and the Sisters have woken two of the three sleeping girls. The last girl remains in the safety of long-sleep while they work on making successful repairs to her heart. She will be waking soon, when waking no longer means death for her.

Vreni laughed to herself. The girls were amazed to have woken up in another time and place. Their new world frightened and fascinated them. It was funny to see them fretting over the creatures trapped inside the television, just like Vreni had done so long ago. She knew she had saved them. If she hadn't killed the Master, they would still be lying in a heap like discarded rag dolls, perhaps forever.

She would teach the girls about their new world and their unique history. They could choose to sleep again, because the Wise Sisters now had complete control of both formulas.

These ideas swam in Vreni's head, making her dizzy. It was all over. She had won a victory for her family and herself. So why, with all this freedom, did she feel as though she was weighed down with lead? All she had ever wanted was to be free to live like everyone else, to travel and love: to live free of secrets.

She flicked absent mindedly through the heavy pages of the family journal that lay open next to her own. The history it held was rich and powerful. The people held within its pages were exceptional and strong. They had spanned centuries and remained resilient against so many challenges. Vreni was proud of her unique history and her strength. Would the cure change everything?

Memories of Vreni's century spun through her mind: images of fashion, cars, technology. Her century had been a time of exponential change, and she felt privileged to have been witness to it. But what might the future hold? Maybe she could stay as she was and keep travelling through time. The thought was tantalizing; she loved the thrill of waking to new and marvellous things.

She looked up at the moon. *I would've thought that by now people would be able to visit there.*

Vreni's eyes refocused as William's reflection appeared in the dark mirror of the tower's windows. Something glinted; he was wearing an amulet like the one her father had worn.

'How can you be wearing that?' Vreni's heart raced.

'Sabina said it was my decision.'

'But I haven't said I'll marry you. We've had *one* date,' she said incredulously.

'Love is the magic, Vreni, and I've chosen to do this, to watch over all this,' he said quietly.

'My soul to keep,' Vreni whispered bitterly.

'No, there'll be no *keeping*. I know how that feels, just like you do. But you'll need my help when everyone starts waking up, and I hope you'll still have time for dancing,' he added, smiling.

She smiled back. 'I'd like that, and I did promise you a dance.'

'Only one,' he laughed, and took her hand, spinning her around.

She touched the amulet. 'What about if, I mean *when*, I take the cure?'

'Then I take this off, I suppose. So is it if or when?'

'I don't know yet. I need more time to decide.'

'Well, we have plenty of that,' he said, rubbing the amulet slowly.

'I'm not sure if I want to miss out on—'

'I know,' William said, smiling. 'The future's too good a place to give up, and now we can think about sharing it. No rush,' he said, squeezing her shoulders.

'No rush,' she agreed, looking up at the moon again. 'I always thought I'd get to go there.'

'Maybe you will.'

'Maybe I will.'

Acknowledgements

269

Thank you to Yvonne Mes, Monique Moy and Isabella Maher for your writerly support. I'm pleased to have had you to share the journey with me.

Declan and Trae Allen are the best monster wranglers, I'm so glad I had their creativity and insight to keep all my scary creatures from getting out of control.

Thank you to Penny, Anthony and the team for you professional insight and guidance on my journey from writer to author.

About the author

Martii Maclean lives in a tin shack by the sea, catching sea-gulls which she uses to make delicious pies. She likes to write weird stories for young people to enjoy. Martii loves going for long bicycle rides with her cat, who always wears aviator goggles to stop her whiskers blowing up into her eyes as they speed down to the beach to search for mermaid eggs.

Visit **martiimaclean.com**

Find out more **about** Martii and her other **stories**.
Share her **blog** and news of upcoming **events**.
Stop in for a **BRAIN SNACK**-creative thoughts and tips for **young writers**.